CONSEQUENCES OF
Secrets!

CONSEQUENCES OF

Secrets!

Jennifer Marie Kent

CITI OF BOOKS

CITIOFBOOKS, INC.
3736 Eubank NE Suite A1
Albuquerque, NM 87111-3579
www.citiofbooks.com

Hotline: 1 (877) 389-2759
Fax: 1 (505) 930-7244

Ordering Information:
Quantity sales. Special discounts are available on quantity purchases by corporations, associations, and others. For details, contact the publisher at the address above.

Printed in the United States of America.

ISBN-13:   Paperback   979-8-89391-358-3
             eBook   979-8-89391-359-0

Library of Congress Control Number: 2024920123

This book is dedicated to:
My family and friends, because without your help,
it would have never been possible.
Without your help, I would have starved to death.
Thank you to every one of you; you literally saved my life

Historical Information

This book opens many years after *The Decision of a Loving Son* came to a sorrowful end. Julia Temperance Brewer grew up in the small southern town, where she raised her daughter. This book rejoins Tempy, who has reached adulthood. As she looks for something she has not known with anyone in a long time, she feels lost and alone. With no one to turn to and no one to help, she must make her own way for the first time in her life.

Tempy doesn't know where she is going or what waits for her when she gets there. It is the most frightening time of her life. What she winds up finding is beyond anything she could have dreamed possible. When her husband forced her to leave her childhood home, Tempy thought he had taken all hope away from her, but the opposite was true; Tempy would find the life she always dreamed was waiting for her. When it looked as though her life was crashing around her, she finds more happiness than she ever knew existed, a type of happiness she could only imagine was possible.

Chapter 1

After living through three of the hardest years of her life, Tempy felt angry and alone as she walked out of the house, she bought from her mother many years before her death. Tempy was heartbroken over the loss of her family's home; she couldn't believe it. Tom Pierce had stolen the house and property out from under her, and to her dismay, the laws of the state were no help; there was nothing legally she could do. When he'd mortgaged the house, he'd had the mortgage company insert a clause that made it possible for him to have a place to live no matter what happened. Tom had cost Tempy everything she loved: her parents' home, her daughter, and now he was trying to take her self-respect.

Tempy wanted to make a fresh start, but she had no clue where she would go or what she would do to keep a roof over her head. No one could tell her what lay ahead in her life. She'd have to figure out the future for herself. She would have to wait a little while to see what destiny had in store for her. Whatever it was, she was ready for a new beginning. It was an exciting but scary time in her life. In fact, she was more scared now than during the twenty years of hell she had lived through with Tom.

Tempy was more than ready for a change. She secretly hoped Tom would not want to be a part of her future, but she had to wait and see how things worked out between them. As she left the house, she began to cry and continued crying uncontrollably the entire drive north to Manchester, Georgia. Her heart was broken, but there was no one around who cared enough to hold her and make sure she was all right.

Tom never asked her what was wrong or tried in any way to comfort her. All he seemed to care about was whether he had a cigarette to smoke. Over the last couple of years, Tom did not care about anything or anyone but cigarettes. He expected her to keep him with a constant supply. Nothing was more important to him than cigarettes; they came before food for the house, and any other necessity of life was seen as a secondary need. It had been the hardest seven years she had ever spent anywhere. She decided she was going to put all the ugliness behind her and start her life over. She wanted to go where nobody knew her or what happened during her life.

Tom made her hate him because of the mental abuse he subjected her to on a daily basis. Her feelings for him had turned from love to what seemed more like hate in the blink of an eye. Tempy knew she had been feeling this way toward him for a while but try as she might to get away from him, she could find no way out. All the fates seemed to conspire to keep her confined to his side.

She had loved and worshipped this man, but after he got sick, she could not stand to be in the same room with him. When Tom went into the operating room, Tempy found out all the dirty, nasty things he had done while he was still in good health. She never dreamed a person who claimed to love someone could hurt her the way he did. What she had discovered about Tom was just mean. How could he take the one thing that meant the most to her and leave her with nothing? She could not understand what she had done to him that gave him the right to treat her the way he had for the last twenty-eight years. She had always thought he loved her, but what she had discovered in his papers showed her the opposite was true. Family members had tried to warn her about Tom, but she would not listen. She could not believe he would hurt her the way everyone predicted.

Tom had mortgaged her family's home for almost three times what it was worth and then refused to make the payments. Tempy had been struggling to keep her family home, but deep down, she knew it was just a matter of time before she lost everything. To make matters worse, there was that clause in the mortgage contract that stated should anything happen to Tom, the mortgage company could and would foreclose on the house. If he were not living in the home, the mortgage company foreclosed, so if Tempy tried to throw him out, she would lose the house. Thanks to his manipulations, he appeared to have a place to live for as long as he wanted. Now he had her where he always said he would leave her, with nothing to fall back on. Property her mother had given her belonged to him. Tempy did not see a lot of options left if something happened to him. Some of what he had set in motion was likely to happen sooner rather than later. That meant it was just a matter of time before she found herself without a place to live if he got behind on the mortgage payments.

Tempy had been unable to find work in the small Georgia town. There had always been some seasonal work here and there, but this year seemed different somehow. None of the companies she had worked for in the past wanted her back. Their feelings toward her made no sense, and she was desperate for an income

As fate would have it, one month, Tom did not get his Social Security, leaving Tempy with no alternative but to approach the mortgage company for a way out. She was looking for something that would help her and not place the stigma of a foreclosure on her parents' home.

Tempy got permission from the mortgage company to have what they call a short sale. When her real estate agent accepted fifty-five thousand dollars for the house and the lot it sat on, the mortgage company jumped at it. Their appraiser told them that was what the house and property were worth. He said his appraisal of the house and property was a guess because nobody in that area ever moved. No one had sold any property in the neighborhood for over forty years, leaving no clue regarding property values in the area.

Tempy also sold the two lots her mother had given her the same day she deeded her the house. They were in her name, and she owned those two lots outright. Tom wasn't entitled to get half the proceeds from that sale, and if she didn't want to sell, she didn't have to. When a contractor offered to buy both lots along with the house and the lot it sat on for $125,000, she thought she had heard the agent wrong when she told her about the sale. She could not believe her turn of luck. She was surprised she got anything for her part of the property.

Tom had gone behind her back and taken out a mortgage three times more than the house and lot was worth. Given the way the house sat on the property, there were not lot of choices about what to do with the land once someone purchased it. When and if someone bought the property and house, they could not get the city to run a sewer line to the property. They would have to build a new house, install a septic tank, and run new lines to handle the house's sewage.

Her house was so upside down, she could not believe someone wanted the property. She found out that when she married Tom, everything Tempy's mother left her became his, and he was able to take out a mortgage without her permission. There was nothing she could do about it. According to her attorney, in the state of Georgia, if a man lived in the house with you, it became his homestead; he was as entitled to the property as the person who inherited the property.

Tom took advantage of the fact he and Tempy had been married years before and used the situation against Tempy to do whatever he pleased to her and the house.

Several months before he mortgaged Tempy's house, Tom was given the property his mother and her husband had owned for years. He purchased another used truck but offered Tempy none of the money from the sale of his parents' property. His family had never honored Tom and Tempy's marriage and felt she had no right to anything from the sale of that property. To them she was a piece of trash and would be treated like any trash blowing down the street.

When Tom was diagnosed with a cyst in the center of his brain, Tempy was given two choices for his care: have the cyst removed or watch him die. Instead, he was left with shortterm memory loss and would tell anyone who asked what he thought they wanted to hear.

He was often heard telling anyone who would listen, "This house belongs to Tempy. Her mother left the house and property to her when she died a few years ago."

Even though Tom admitted the house belonged to Tempy, it was too late. Everyone saw him as competent to do business before surgery, which made whatever Tempy said or did irrelevant. What it amounted to was the contract tied her to what he had done as her husband. She found she had no recourse available to her. She could not press charges against Tom for signing her name to give the mortgage company permission to place a mortgage. They claimed he was now unable to help a lawyer with his own defense.

Despite everything he had done, there was nothing anyone could do to keep Tom from getting the house. Tempy had no choice but to get the mortgage out of his name or move. She was on her own and knew she was in a losing battle. If she did not sell her property when the house sold, she would have nowhere to live and no way to support herself. From the beginning of their relationship, Tom had planned to leave Tempy in a bad position. His relatives knew he was planning to force her to live with her daughter, Lizzie, or live under the bridge that stretched across the river at the edge of town. It was difficult to keep his plans from coming to fruition, but Tempy worked hard to find a buyer and find herself an acceptable way out.

Tempy's heart was breaking. She cried a few tears for the old house and neighborhood. It was hard for her to take; she had always called this home. With the reality of the situation, she forced herself to come to terms with losing her home.

Tempy's feelings for the house, the memories she accumulated, and what the house meant to her made it hard to accept, but at this point in her life, she was ready for a new beginning. Some things in her life she had control over, but this, she did not.

For many years, Tempy wanted to get more out of life, but she never knew what she was looking for. She knew she couldn't find her heart's desire in Jacksonville, Georgia. Her dreams would not come true, stuck in the same place she called home since the day she was born. She heard others tell stories about there being more in the world waiting for her; she needed to stop letting her fears control her and go after her heart's desire. It would not be easy. In the last few months, she realized nobody would hand her what she wanted in life. She had to go after what she wanted to make something out of the rest of her life.

Tempy promised herself she would make a fresh start. She was curious to find out before she got too old to care about such things, what she missed waiting and not acting on her desires. Still a somewhat young woman, she believed in her heart it was possible for her to start over and for her to find the kind of happiness she always dreamed awaited her.

She was young enough she could still make for herself the life she always wanted. She could find a man who loved her for herself, not for her money. Tom left her with nothing. He had taken her home, her self-respect, and everyone she had ever loved. It would be hard at first; she would have to begin her journey as though she had begun it for the first time.

Tom always told her if the two of them separated, he would make sure she was penniless. In Tempy's naivety, she never believed he would do it. She found out the hard way she had been wrong about him, about a lot of things. When everything he had done to her came to light, she could not believe how blind she had been.

She didn't want another man in her life at this moment, maybe ever. She could not give anyone else the chance to take advantage of her. For the first time in a lot of years, she liked the direction her life was taking. All she wanted was to make a life for herself without someone's help. Look where a man's help got her. For all intents and purposes, she was homeless. She had nowhere to go and no one could help her figure things out. It was like living in a horror movie, but through the adversity, she gained strength and decided she would make a better life for herself. She just had to figure things out. When she figured out where she wanted to call home, she would start to make her dreams come true.

Chapter 2

As Julia Temperance Brewer Pierce left Jacksonville, Georgia, that bright morning, she had no clue where she'd be when the sun went down that day. She had no way of taking care of herself, and it frightened her. She only wanted to get as far away as she could from the man she had lived with the last twenty-eight years. She was driven by a need to put distance between them.

She could not understand how things had changed; before, they were in love, but now it was ugly and bitter. She wished to feel better about herself. Tom had messed with her mind so much she could not tell when someone was being nice to her. She thought everyone she met was out to get her. For the last five years, she distrusted everyone she met. She could not believe she had let somebody turn her into the person she saw when she looked in the mirror. She disliked this person, but she had to protect herself from the lies associated with her childhood home.

Her life had gotten so bad; in those last few years, she would beg God not to let people come to visit. She did not like the way they treated her. Everyone thought she was a shy girl who would take anything off anyone and never say one word. People still thought she would let them do whatever they could to her, and she would stand by and take their abuse. It was not just neighbors; it was friends and family as well. She had let people do this to her since she was young, and no one thought she would ever change. But in the last couple of months, people found out she was no longer a pushover. She came out of the corner her family and friends had pushed her into. She would not take their abuse anymore and did not care how mad anyone got. She had to take up for herself, and for the first time in her life, she found the courage to speak out.

Before Tempy left, she tried to ask Tom if he wanted to go with her to start her life over. She was embarrassed to stay in Jacksonville. Everyone there knew her, and she did not want to answer any questions about what had happened.

He always changed the subject and never gave her a straight answer to her question. He liked to be in charge. He wanted to know where they were going and where they would live. She didn't know where she was going but knew it was not where she was now.

For months, she hoped he would not want to go with her. To her delight, after she picked up the U-Haul truck she rented, he said he'd rather go stay with his sister in Manchester.

His decision made Tempy happy beyond belief. She could do what she pleased without someone watching her or questioning her. He and his family had accused Tempy of every ugly thing imaginable. These accusations made Tempy feel dirty. She longed to be as far as she could from them. When he said he wanted to go to his sister's, Tempy wanted to jump up and down and clap, but she had to sit there and act as though it disappointed her.

Tom talked to his sisters and his children on the phone almost daily. In those conversations, he told them Tempy brought other men into the house and had sex while he sat in the kitchen and listened. He told these stories so many times, she felt dirty; she wanted to stand in the shower for hours and wash all the filth away. She could not help but dream of a better life for herself, that was clean and pure and worth holding onto. She wished so many times she could kill herself and get out of the hell that was living with him.

Tempy always heard if two people wanted to be together and laughed together, their lives would fly by. Her life was miserable; one year to her was more like ten. She told this to a couple of people, but no one suggested how to change things for the better.

"My life is like having a press on my shoulders," she said, "and I am being thrown into a hole with the dirt being pushed in on top of me, while someone stands on my shoulders, jumping up and down, packing my body into the ground. The pressure increases, and I feel like I'm suffocating as I attempt to free myself from my prison."

Tom told Tempy he wanted to stay with Beth until she found a place where they could resettle. When she found a home, she could come back to Manchester and get him, and he would move in. Tempy didn't like that he was going to live with Beth; he did this once before, and it turned out badly for them, but she also thought it was better for him to go to Beth's and not with her. She was going to be free to be herself, not someone somebody else wanted her to be.

Tempy knew this was going to be a repeat of the past. She knew anyone could convince Tom to do what they wanted. As she drove, she cried a few tears for the miserable events she knew deep in her soul were going to come to pass.

Tom's health was getting worse. He could barely walk, and he never signed his name in the same manner twice anymore. Tom was like living with a small child in a man's body. Tempy could not stand him for what he cost her and the way he treated her. Tempy wondered if she'd find someone who loved her as a person. She wanted to experience what it felt like to be with someone who loved her and treated her right.

When Tempy and Tom arrived in Manchester, it was lunchtime. They found a small restaurant that served down-home meals. After they ate, she would take him to Beth's. As they were eating, Tempy asked Tom if this was what he wanted to do. He confirmed that he wanted to stay with his sister until Tempy got a job and found a place for them to live.

Tempy had to trust his family would allow her the time she needed to get settled. A little voice in the back of her mind kept telling her, "Be careful. You're living on borrowed time. You have to watch these people. If they smile at you when you drop him off, you're about to get a knife in the back, so wear your armor tight around yourself."

After they finished eating, they got back into the U-Haul. They didn't speak as she drove him to Beth's. When they got to his sister's, Tom asked her to let him off at the end of the driveway. He knew that Tempy and Beth disliked each other. He wanted no trouble for her when she dropped him off. He got out of the truck, and she watched while he walked down the driveway before resuming her journey, alone.

She felt a little sad about leaving him; she couldn't help it. She lived with Tom for almost thirty years. During that time, he became an enormous part of her life. Her sadness gave way to a sense of calmness while she watched him walk away; it was liberating. Tempy wanted it to be his choice; she did not want to take care of him anymore. His family would accuse her of abandoning him. Her heart fluttered every time she wondered what happened. She was aware it was a matter of time before they made him divorce her and have Tempy pay him a substantial settlement just to get away from him.

When Tempy pulled over to let Tom out of the U-Haul, a black SUV passed them. They didn't pay much attention to the vehicle driving down the small country road. Tempy and Tom had run a diesel repair shop and were accustomed to seeing SUVs and large cars around the area. Also, Beth's late husband owned a body shop, and SUVs were common in his business.

As Tempy drove away, she let out a sigh of relief. She was over the moon that Tom decided to stay in Manchester. With him out of the truck, she could not help noticing the relief in her shoulders. She felt as though a monkey had jumped off her back. She knew she wanted to get away from him but didn't realize until he was gone just how much she had grown to hate him. Her heart was at peace, and for the first time in an awfully long time, she could breathe.

As she drove, she thought, *Where am I going? What will become of me?* She had no idea what her future held in store for her or even where she wanted to go. When she stopped for gas, she found a brochure for South Carolina on the counter of the convenience store. As she stood waiting to pay for her gas, she noticed another black SUV sitting in the parking lot. Tempy realized she had seen a lot of the same model

SUV while she was travelling today. There were so many of them on the roads, so Tempy never gave the SUV another thought.

She got back into the U-Haul and headed up I-85 through Georgia and into South Carolina. Pendleton was an area she had been fascinated with, ever since she found out her ancestors settled in that part of South Carolina after they left North Carolina. She let her mind wander to the possibilities and realized Pendleton was as good a place as any to start over. With Tom's constant putdowns, name calling, and accusations the last few years, she wanted to be anywhere but Georgia. She saw moving to Pendleton as a chance to experience what her ancestors saw when they moved south. She looked forward to finding out what kind of place her ancestors called home.

Traffic was so bad going through Atlanta, it slowed Tempy down for four hours. The trip through Georgia took longer than normal. With traffic so horrible, it was late in the evening when Tempy reached Pendleton.

After driving for such a long period of time, she started getting tired. She intended to stop in Atlanta for the evening but realized she wanted to go a little longer. She wanted to get as far away from Manchester as she could.

A little after dark, she found a small bed and breakfast and checked herself into the family-owned establishment. While she was standing at the registration counter, she and the manager struck up a conversation.

Tempy told her, "I'm looking for work in the area. I'm considering calling Pendleton my new home."

"We'd be glad to have you in our friendly little town," the manager said. "We think you'll like Pendleton so much, you'll be happy to call the area home."

As she turned around and started toward her room, the manager handed her a copy of the day's newspaper and a black book she kept that contained a lot of the better job listings for the Pendleton area. She took the key and the newspaper and followed the bellhop towards her room. That evening, she scanned the local paper for jobs in the area. She also looked at the listings the manager had given her from her personal black book; those jobs paid a lot more than the ones in the newspaper.

Tempy decided to start looking for a job the next morning. She had to find work immediately if she wanted to stay in Pendleton. She had her heart set on the area to make her new life. She was free of Tom and his controlling influence. She could find friends and work with whoever she pleased, without worrying about Tom, who always accused her of being unfaithful to him.

Tempy had no intentions of ever going back to Jacksonville. Her memories of her hometown were just too difficult to deal with right now. There was too much pain involved. Memories of Taylor and the home Tom lost were just too much. Everywhere she looked, she was reminded of what she lost. Would she and Taylor ever find their way back to each other?

Every memory of that Georgia town was bad. She had once loved her hometown and was proud to call Jacksonville home. Now it was painful to even think of the town. Tempy needed time to heal and saw no way she could come to terms with her pain and loss in the one place that had caused her so much grief.

Chapter 3

Tempy woke up early to start the first morning of her adventure. The sky was a bright shade of blue as she prepared to explore what waited for her out there. She was overjoyed with the prospects she saw awaiting her in this new town. She looked forward to creating a life for herself there and was ready to change into the woman she always knew existed inside her.

She lay in bed, listening to the birds outside singing their joyful songs and the other guests milling about in the hallway on the other side of her door. As she lay in her warm, comfy bed, she began to figure out how to start a life in this unfamiliar place, a place where she knew nobody. She got up, took a shower, got dressed, and strolled out of her room, ready to face the day and life head on.

As she walked out onto the balcony, she was struck by the beautiful scenery around the bed and breakfast. It had been dark when she checked in, and she could not see the view, but what she saw this morning was the most beautiful place she had ever seen. One day, Tempy wanted a home with a view like this one. She doubted there was another place on earth that could be any more perfect.

She was looking forward to starting her new life and to whatever happened next to her. It could only be better than the horror she left behind. Tom made her live in sheer misery for a long time, and now she was ready for a change in her luck.

After her brief walk, Tempy felt alive. Everything around her looked better than she remembered it from the day before. She went up to her room and decided to go downstairs and have breakfast. As she turned towards the door that went out into the hallway, she caught sight of a newspaper and what turned out to be a help-wanted poster. Someone had slipped them under her door while she was out. Tempy thought it could have been the night manager. She had no clue that anyone else might be helping her find a way to stay in the area.

Tempy didn't suspect someone in Pendleton was making all of this happen for her. James Braden, a friend of the B&B's night manager, wanted to help Tempy in any way he could. He even asked two men who worked for him to follow her from a discreet distance. They began watching her before she left Jacksonville. When she stopped at the convenience store, one of the men followed her into the store and planted the pamphlet on the counter where she would be sure to find it. As she made her way into Pendleton, the evening before, the people responsible for the events of the day were already aware she made her way into town. They were trying to get her to come to the bank and apply for a job. Once she got there and interviewed, they could give her the position they had been holding for her the last few weeks.

It had been a tall, dark-haired man who slipped both the newspaper and the helpwanted poster under Tempy's door while she was out. These people hoped she would see the poster and call the number on it. They wanted Tempy to come to Pendleton and interview at the bank. If she applied for the job, it was hers for the taking.

She carried the newspaper and help-wanted poster downstairs so she could go over them while she ate her breakfast. After she sat down, she took the poster out, read it again, and decided to call the bank first.

Her waiter came over and asked what she wanted for breakfast; with a big grin, she said, "Two blueberry pancakes, bacon, not crispy but not limp either, somewhere in between the two, and coffee."

"Cream and sugar?"

"Yes, thank you."

"It will be out in a few minutes."

"Thank you."

As the waiter stepped away, she looked over the help-wanted poster more closely. There was a contact number on the poster to learn more about the job.

Tempy had never worked in a bank before but thought it might be fun to apply for a different kind of job. She dialed the number on the poster. A woman answered the phone. Tempy introduced herself and told the woman she was calling regarding the help-wanted poster. The woman told her the position was in the accounting department at South Carolina Bank and Trust.

"South Carolina Bank and Trust is looking for someone to work in their Accounting Department. If you're interested, you need to come in and talk with our owner and bank manager as part of the hiring process. The position in accounting requires attending board meetings with the owner once every three months. The person will also work closely with the bank manager. He and the person in accounting must be able to work well together because they will be together a lot of the time. It will be their job to identify problems before they get to the owner's desk.

"That sounds fine," Tempe said. "I'd like to set up an interview."

"When can you come in?" the woman asked. "Is one o'clock this afternoon too soon for you?"

"One this afternoon will be fine with me."

Tempy could not believe how lucky she was. When she discovered the help-wanted poster that morning, it was like a sign from above that she was taking her life in the right direction. She never expected to get an interview the same day she called. Prospective applicants often must wait days for an interview if they are called back at all. Tempy thought about how fortunate she had been to find that poster. She could relax for a while before getting ready for the interview.

She finished her breakfast, returned to her room, and changed her clothes. She would sit beside the pool for a little while, relax, and read the paper. She wanted to find out what she could about the area.

While she was lying beside the pool, she happened across a story about the Genealogical Society in Anderson. The writer described some of the material they had gathered through the years. One of their earliest supporters had passed and left them a large amount of memorabilia, which interested her, since her own family had once lived in the area.

Her ancestors, John Adams, and John Calhoun, lived in Pendleton until Georgia opened up to settlers after the War of 1812. When the war was over and the Native Americans were removed from their lands, they allowed settlers to move south, opening up a frontier for others to follow. It would not take long for entire families to follow those first brave souls to parts of the country no one had seen before. They found gold and, to their dismay, more of those dreaded Native Americans.

She was hoping she could get some answers to her questions. The more she read, the more interested she became. She was eager to get a peek at what the Genealogical Society's patron had donated. Maybe it could assist her with her own research, or at least bring her closer to getting through the brick wall she discovered involving one of her forefathers.

John Adams was a genuine mystery; there was no information about who his parents were. You could find clues, but no one from either of the families knew who his parents had been or where he came from. He apparently fell out of a tree at twenty years of age and became an enormous part of the Adams and Calhoun families. There must be a clue somewhere about who gave him life.

He was a genuine challenge for her. She now had the opportunity to use the training she received years ago in the field of genealogy research. She decided to visit the Genealogical Society later in the week. For now, she wanted to relax and prepare for her interview as an accountant at the bank, which she had trained for and worked as for years.

While she sat by the pool, she read the story again to give her an idea about what questions to ask about her ancestors. She needed a fresh set of eyes to look at the information she had gathered. Maybe they could find a clue to what she was missing. Was there something in her notes she did not see because she was so close to what she had gathered? Over time, she had become blind to the way the research was leading her.

The story said John Adams and John Calhoun had come to the area in the early 1800s. Adams and Calhoun were her fourth and fifth great-grandfathers, and anything giving any kind of details about these two men interested her.

She put the story down and went back to her room to get ready for her interview. She did not want to be late and make a bad impression.

Before she left for the bank, she took her poodles outside one more time, so they could get a little more exercise. They were the light of her life and had been for a long time. Those three dogs held a large part of her heart, and she would do whatever it took to protect them.

Chapter 4

The previous night, Tempy read an article in a magazine she found lying face down on the nightstand; it described how eight years ago, South Carolina Bank and Trust had been on the brink of total bankruptcy. Everybody who worked for the bank thought it was their lucky day when a forty-seven-year-old businessman decided to purchase the bank. He expected it would be a challenge to run a bank. It was different from any of his other businesses. No one knew where he came from, but to them, he had been sent from a higher power. With his purchase of the bank, the city of Pendleton was given a boost of cash and was able to keep one of the oldest banks in the state open.

According to the magazine article, James had been in agriculture before moving to Pendleton but then sought a change of occupation. He had had some serious shakeups over the last few decades. He did not think one more change in his life would kill him. He had found that adversity had a way of making him stronger.

James explained he was looking for a change and wanted to make a difference in people's lives. A bank looked attractive and seemed to call to him. The day he stepped into the bank, he heard one of the tellers say her boss was looking for someone to purchase the bank. It seemed to him a sign from heaven; South Carolina Bank and Trust was where destiny had led him to settle down.

Tempy looked through the article for a picture of James, but there was none. She found that a little unusual, since there was a picture of the branch manager, Shawn Mitchell, and the head teller, Brandi

Minor. Wouldn't you expect a person who changes his profession to want the world to give him the credit? Wouldn't he want everyone in town to know who made this possible?

When James came to Pendleton, he decided to settle down. In the twenty years before moving there, he lived many different places, but none of them made him want to stick around longer than a few months. He decided he would create a new chapter in his life there in Pendleton. No one in Pendleton suspected where James came from. But after he had been there awhile, he made a home for himself and became a respected member of the community.

James promised himself he would never become involved with another woman, other than those he worked with. The women in his old life had caused him too many problems. He decided to keep things convenient for himself. He would not become involved with another woman, at least for the near future. Many women over the last eight years were interested in James on an intimate level, but he would let them get close. Every time a woman wanted to date him or showed any interest in him, he would shut her down immediately.

He would tell the women who tried to get close to him, "I'm sorry. I only have eyes for one woman, and as long as she doesn't want me, I'm not interested in getting to know anyone else."

He had been married twice before but only wanted one person. He was willing to wait forever for her to come to him.

Over the last eight years, his decision to stay away from other women had worked well for him, but James's world was about to change. He and Shawn Mitchell had pulled strings in the last couple of months to make sure Temperance Pierce got to Pendleton. His associates, Bruce Henry and Christopher Parker, put everything in place to make things happen the way they wanted. They followed Tempy to make sure nothing bad happened to her.

James had pulled some strings back in Jacksonville to enable Tempy to leave her old life and town behind, forever. One of his people bought her old family home. James made certain she got to Atlanta that Monday afternoon and made it to Pendleton later that evening. He was looking forward to visiting her but being with a woman terrified him. He had devoted a lot of cash, energy, and time into getting her to where she was, right this second. He did not want to do something now that would send her running away from him forever. He realized he had to be careful of what he said to her because she might catch on before he was ready to disclose his secret.

The woman Tempy spoke with that morning said to come to the bank and ask to speak with a young lady named Brandi Minor.

Tempy walked into the bank and went over to the teller counter. She smiled at the first teller and said, "I am here to interview for accounting position. Can I speak to Brandi Minor?"

As she spoke, two of the other tellers turned and gave each other a strange look. Tempy was happy to have a job interview but wondered what that look was all about. It never dawned on her there may be something going on.

The teller handed Tempy a clipboard with a bunch of papers on it and told her to have a seat in the corner and fill out the job application. She had never seen that many forms associated with a job. She never dreamed that working in a bank involved so much paperwork.

After a little while, the first teller came back and told Tempy, "Brandi stepped to the back for a few minutes. She wanted me to apologize to you for the delay. While you are waiting for her to finish, is there anything I can get you?"

"No, I am all right. Thanks anyway."

"You're welcome; would you like a bottle of water or something cold to drink while you wait?"

"A bottled water sounds good. Thank you."

The teller walked over to the bank's break room and came back with an ice-cold bottle of water. She handed it to Tempy and reminded her to finish the paperwork. Tempy sat back down and continued filling out the papers.

James Braden was in his office when Tempy walked into the bank. His office was in the corner of the lobby of the bank. Large panes of glass surrounded the office, which made it possible for everyone to see him when the curtains were open, as they were today. The thick curtains were usually closed for privacy, but that afternoon, they were open.

James didn't care that everyone could see into his office that day; he wanted to see Tempy when she walked in. He stared at her as she filled out the paperwork, but he was discreet and didn't let anyone see him. He could not wait to get this interview started. He was excited and scared at the same time. He was afraid he would mess up, and she would find out what was going on before he could explain everything to her. He thought Tempy could not handle the truth about him. He was afraid if she found out his secret, she'd get mad and walk out before he got the chance to tell her the truth about what happened all those years ago.

Tempy overheard customers talking about the change in the atmosphere around the bank. Many of them had been coming into the bank since James purchased the struggling business years ago. His curtains were never open during the day. He was a known recluse. Everyone who came into the bank wondered why the curtains were open.

"What is going on at the bank that makes today so different from any other day?" people asked. To everyone who walked into the bank they could tell that something was going on today. There's something a little off in the way James is dealing with the day-to-day operation of the bank. Any other time when customers came in to deposit their checks, the curtains were closed.

Tempy tried to ignore these comments and focus on finishing her application, but she was finding it difficult to keep her mind on the paperwork.

Tempy looked up and saw James in his office; she thought he was a good-looking, middle-aged man. As she sat there waiting to talk with him, she could not help feeling she had met him somewhere before. She got a powerful sense of déjà vu every time she looked up at him. There was something familiar about him. But she had never been to South Carolina before in her life. The more she looked at him, the stronger her feelings got. Where could she have met him before? She wondered if maybe she went through Pendleton with Tom many years before, when he drove a truck, but that could not be it. She and Tom never stayed in one place long enough to meet anybody new.

Tempy had this sense of déjà vu, but she could not figure out why. She could not shake the feelings she was having, but she had no idea where she might have met him before. She decided to figure it out at some point, but for the time being, she needed to concentrate on the job interview.

She filled out the forms, privacy information, and approval for the bank to run a background check on her. From time to time, she found herself staring at him instead of working on the application. She got so distracted by him, she got up and took another seat, so she would not keep staring.

No one else knew James opened those curtains so he could see Tempy when she arrived for her interview. He was so excited about seeing her, he could not wait for her interview to begin. He was trying his best to act normal, but he was having a hard time with her sitting just on the other side of the glass. He thought his heart would break when she got up and moved out of his line of sight.

After a while, Tempy walked over and let the teller know she finished the paperwork. After she sat down, Brandi came out of the back, walked over to Tempy, and introduced herself.

"I hope I haven't kept you waiting too long," she said. "I got tied up with another customer."

"No problem," Tempy said. "I filled out all the papers you had for me."

Brandi took the forms, stuck them into a folder, and went into James's office. A few minutes later, he called Shawn Mitchell, the branch manager, to let him know he was ready to start the interview. Brandi came out of the office and told her it would only be a few more minutes.

Tempy could feel the excitement and anxiety building in her chest. She was quite nervous and hoped she would do all right with this interview. She had a lot riding on how she impressed these two men. Her future depended on it.

Brandi showed Tempy into James's office and introduced her to James and Shawn. Tempy shook their hands, and when she shook James's hand, she felt a rush of excitement. She could feel her cheeks flushing and realized the temperature in the room increased several degrees. She hoped no one else noticed her reaction. She did not understand what was going on with her or why she was having such a reaction to him. She only had that kind of reaction one time before in her entire life; only one man made her feel that way: Taylor Michaels.

James wanted Shawn involved with this interview to keep him on track and moving towards his goal: hiring Julia Temperance Brewer Pierce to work in the Accounting Department. He got her there; now he needed to get through this interview without giving away too much about himself. They both knew Tempy was not just a random person off the street who applied for the accounting job.

James knew if he kept Shawn between himself and Tempy, he would not let James give away his secrets. He could not afford for her to figure him out before he was ready to disclose his secret identity. He remembered from when they were kids, she had an uncanny ability to pick up on certain things people did. He was worried that she might pick up on his longing to be with her with every fiber of his being.

Tempy had no problem having Shawn take part in interviewing her. She was just over the moon to be there. This job meant a lot to her and her future, but she would not let it show. She had done accounting-related jobs her entire adult life This job was no different, but there was a lot more responsibility associated with working in a bank. She wanted to do well in this interview because she needed a job. Sure, she had the money she got from the sale of her parents' property, but if she got this job, she could put that money aside in case she needed something to fall back on.

"So, Tempy, what have you heard about our bank?" James asked to begin the interview.

"I haven't heard anything about the bank," she said, explaining, "I'm new in town. I only arrived in the area last night. However, I read in an article in Newsweek that the bank was on the brink of bankruptcy when you purchased it eight years ago."

"Yes, that is true; it was. So what accounting procedures are you familiar with?"

James was trying in the worst way to keep down the conversation between himself and Tempy. He tried to keep the interview about the job and not carry on too much conversation with her. He knew she might recognize his voice if he said too much to her. This left James to conduct the interview that afternoon with brief questions so he could try to disguise his voice.

"I am proficient in all forms of accounting procedures: accounts payable, accounts receivable, payroll, reconciliations, and sales tax. I was given the privilege of doing some consulting for several clients. I find it comforting to help people plan for their futures and retirement. I've helped people understand the risks involved when taking part of their 401(k) too soon. A broker might not tell his client that taking their money early might not be the best thing for them to do. Most brokerage firms do not tell their clients about the 10 percent penalty the Internal Revenue Service charges if they cash out their IRA or 401(k) before reaching a certain age. These brokers are only interested in the fees they collect from their clients, not what it might cost their clients when it comes time to pay their taxes."

"Is there anything in your past that would keep you from working in a bank?"

"No, nothing I know of. I've never stolen anything in my life. I've never been dishonest with anyone."

Shawn chimed in, "There is one thing I must ask you before we go any further."

"What is that Mr. Mitchell?"

"If someone asks you to deal with information of a private and personal nature, can you keep that information to yourself?"

"Do you mean, can I keep secrets?"

Tempy could not help smiling and even laughing aloud; she had been keeping secrets her entire life. This was an easy question. She could not help remembering her youth and the secrets she kept from that time.

"Yes, that is what I am asking you."

James sat and stared at her, remembering when Tempy was more than happy to keep secrets. He got mad when he thought she told someone about their most intimate times together. He hoped she didn't see him smiling when she told Shawn she was keeping many of those secrets today.

"Is this a phone number we can use to reach you?"

"Yes, it is, or you can call me at the bed and breakfast, where I am staying for the time being. I arrived in Pendleton last night and haven't found a place to live yet."

"OK, Tempy, thank you for coming in today."

James had been like that since the day he purchased the bank. His conversations with everyone were short and sweet, and he got to the point without mincing words. He did not like having lengthy conversations with anyone. He did not want to give anyone the opportunity to get too close to him or to spend too much time with him. He was afraid if someone got too close, they might recognize his face and figure out who he was. Before James came to Pendleton, he underwent a lot of plastic surgery to change the features of his face.

His surgeon told him point blank, "If a person from your past looks at you long enough, they might figure out who you are. If they see the scars behind your ears, they may be able to tell you had plastic surgery.

It will be best to stay to yourself and keep your dealings with other people to a minimum."

He never let people look at him in the eye. Every time Tempy caught his gaze, he would turn his head away. When their eyes met, she could see they were the prettiest green eyes she ever saw. James knew it would be hard to hide the details of his past from her. She thought he was being too cautious. She could tell he was trying to hide something from her, but she could not figure out what.

James had closed himself off from other people. After going to all the trouble of getting Tempy to town, to his dismay, he was still having problems allowing her to get too close to him. He did not want anyone getting around the many walls he built around himself. He avoided people, so they would not ask him questions he could not give them the answers to. If anybody figured out the answers, it could place his life in danger. He had worked hard, and only a handful of people ever got close enough to learn about his past.

For the time being, he would keep his identity a secret from Tempy. James never socialized with anyone outside the office. His life was the way he wanted it to be. He knew many of the women who worked with him wanted to be more than just business associates. He did not want to get involved with anyone, at least for a little while longer. When he was ready, the women at the bank would be mad, but James only had eyes for one woman, and he was doing everything in his power to get her where he wanted her.

James had no intention of letting anyone come between his desire to have Temperance Brewer in his life again; he would do whatever it took to get her back in his life. This time, he hoped it would be forever, not just an afternoon here and there, but something they could build a future on.

Chapter 5

With the interview over, Tempy rose to her feet and shook hands with Shawn. He said, "Tempy, we will call you with our decision when we decide who is right for the position."

"Thank you, Mr. Mitchell," she said. "I will await your call."

James walked her to the door, and before she went out, they shook hands, and she said, "Thank you for your time this afternoon, Mr. Braden."

"You are most welcome, Tempy," James said; he wanted to confess to her who he was, but he had to let things stay the way they were, for a while longer.

After the interview, Tempy walked around Pendleton for a little while. During her walk, she found a self-storage unit and decided to rent a car after unloading the truck.

While unloading her belongings from the U-Haul into storage, Tempy decided to go to Anderson the next morning to visit the Genealogical Society. She wanted to see for herself what she could find out about her ancestors. She would love to figure out her own genealogy. She was curious to see what kind of information the Genealogical Society had gathered on John Adams and John Calhoun.

Tempy had worked on her family's genealogy for almost twenty years, but she couldn't find much information on these two ancestors. Over the years, two of her great-aunts said the Adamses came from

Anderson, South Carolina. Tempy wanted to see if she could find any information about these two men. She hoped they had more than she found back in Jacksonville at their library.

She was so nervous when she got up, she decided to just have a light breakfast before she left for Anderson. She left about nine that morning and drove slowly from Pendleton to Anderson, so she could familiarize herself with the area a little more. She arrived at the Genealogical Society office a little after eleven. It was an impressive two-story building. Tempy could feel a knot in her stomach and realized she couldn't eat anything before she went inside. She was too nervous. She wanted to see what they had found concerning her two ancestors.

When she walked in, she could not believe all the material they had from the area's first settlers. The Anderson Genealogical Society displayed artifacts that did their ancestors a great honor. She walked up to the counter where two women were sorting through some artifacts.

"Excuse me," she said. "I was wondering if one of you might help me find some information."

"Yes, ma'am, we will try. What is it you need help with?"

"I am looking for information on John Adams and John Calhoun. I read an article that said you had assembled a wide assortment of information on these men."

One of the workers almost dropped the artifact she was cleaning. Tempy was startled by this reaction to the mention of her ancestor's names.

One of the other employees asked, "Did you say you want any information on John Adams and John Calhoun?"

"Yes, I did."

"Have you verified your lineage to these men?"

"Yes, I have. I am a member of the Daughters of the American Revolution, and we did research on Joseph Calhoun, the father of John Calhoun. I am descended from him in a straight line; I can confirm the brothers as well and one of his sisters. I have done a lot of research on these two families."

"Do you know you are the first of their descendants to come looking for any information about them?"

"No, but it doesn't surprise me in the least. My family has always thought John Adams went to Georgia straight from North Carolina. Two of my great-aunts stated in a newspaper article, the family came to South Carolina first and then traveled to Georgia; they helped found Pike County when the territory opened in the1820s."

"You don't have a heart problem, do you?"

"No," Tempy said. "Why, do I look ill?"

The workers all laughed at Tempy. She was trying to lighten up the atmosphere in the room, but everybody was so serious. They all looked at her in disbelief; they couldn't believe she was standing there asking them these questions.

"No, you don't seem to be ill. You might want to sit down when we show you what we have on these two men. We can show you what they owned before they left for parts unknown. Up until now, we had no clue where they went when they left Pendleton."

Tempy sat down and began talking to one lady while other members of the society found the information they had on these two gentlemen. They introduced her as the director of the Society. The employees showed Tempy what patrons had given to them over the years.

"First, we have these two bank account books which they left here at the Genealogical Society over 197 years ago. Our Genealogical Society has been using the funds in the accounts to keep the properties and the principal homestead in the style it enjoyed since the Civil War. We were lucky that Sherman missed these two houses on his march to Savannah. Everything out there is still just like John Calhoun and John Adams left it.

"We don't know how much was here in 1820 monetary amounts. Someone at the bank in Pendleton knows what's in them, but we do not. It was less tempting for us to not know how much money is in the bank. That way, there's less temptation to be tempted to use any of the money from the accounts." It is only human nature to want to use money that is not being used by anyone. To some it would be easy to do, and nobody would ever know, right.

While Tempy and the director talked, one worker went to their computer in the back of the room and pulled up a link to the Daughters of the American Revolution. After a few minutes, they confirmed Tempy's lineage. When the director learned she was telling the truth, she handed her both bank books.

"According to all our information, you are the rightful owner of everything out there. Your lineage entitles you to everything that belonged to those two men. John Adams and John Calhoun owned two houses, two other buildings in town, and some land, as well as the two bank books."

She didn't have time to check out the deeds. She figured the genealogy staff gave her an insignificant amount of land and maybe two rundown old houses. She never imagined she would be lucky enough to own the two homes her ancestors lived in. She thanked the ladies at the Genealogical Society, stuck the books and deeds into her purse, and left.

As she walked out of the building, she could not believe it. She had not expected to find any information on her ancestors. To her surprise, these ladies gave her everything belonging to these two men. She was holding more than she had ever dreamed possible. She found more information on her two grandfathers that morning than she had ever found in the library in Jacksonville or anywhere on the internet in the last ten years.

She got into her car, started the engine, and just sat there for a few minutes, letting the information the staff had given her sink in. As she was driving back to Pendleton, she realized she had forgotten all about being hungry. Her stomach was not registering with her brain; she still needed to get something to eat. She wondered if this was true or if someone was playing a cruel joke on her. She needed someone to tell her if the documents the staff had given her were real. If they were,

Tempy had hit the information gold mine, but who could help her? After all, she was new in town and didn't know anyone yet. The only people she knew were at the bank and the employees of the bed and breakfast.

Tempy needed someone to tell her what she had as far as the bank accounts were concerned. Staff at the Genealogical Society had told her the bank was in Pendleton, but they never told her which bank. The staff told her she would have to get any information about those accounts from the bank the men had deposited their money with. They had made it clear it would be up to her to contact the bank which owned them.

Tempy did not want Tom anywhere near what she had found concerning her great grandfathers. She felt she had inherited this on her own, and he should not be able to share in her good fortune. It had been Tom's choice to stay in Manchester with Beth. Tempy had nothing to do with what he chose to do. As she was told on many occasions, he was a grown man and made his own decisions. She would do everything in her power to keep him from finding out about the Adams/Calhoun inheritance, or die trying. She did not want her new life to hold the same hell as the one she had just gotten away from.

It was going to be a long time before Tempy could trust a man again.

Chapter 6

James and Shawn met in James's office so no one else could hear them discuss Tempy's interview. They didn't want anyone to know they were giving Tempy the position in accounting because James knew her in the past. As far as anyone else needed to know, she was offered the position because of her background. Shawn admitted she had more than enough experience for the position. He could find no problems with hiring Tempy as the accounting director.

"Are you sure you want to do this, Jim?" Shawn asked.

"Yes," he said. "I didn't do all this just to get her here and not hire her."

"When do you want me to call her and offer her the position?"

"After lunch tomorrow. We cannot afford for anyone to get suspicious about what is going on."

"Yes, sir. You got it, Jim. I will take care of everything for you."

"Thank you, Shawn."

"Is there anything else?"

"Yes, I want the condo fixed up this afternoon. I want to offer it to her to live in while she gets established in her new surroundings. I don't want her feeling like I did eight years ago when I moved here. She will need friends. I can be her friend from a distance, for a while. Take care of her for me, Shawn."

"You got it, Jim."

"Thank you. After that, make sure she has everything she needs. Take care of any obstacle she runs into."

"When do you plan on telling her about yourself?"

"I don't know; I haven't planned that far in advance."

"I'd like to have a say in when and how she finds out about you and what we have done to get her here."

"I suppose that will be all right. I already hurt this woman bad enough. I never want to see pain like that on her face ever again. I already put her through enough pain in her life. I hurt her enough over the years for one lifetime and many others."

"Do you think she can keep a secret?"

"She told you she's been keeping secrets her entire life. She was not lying about that. Tempy has kept some of my biggest secrets her entire life. At one point, I was her secret, or she was my secret, whichever way you want to put it."

"OK, I will call her about one o'clock tomorrow afternoon."

"Thank you, Shawn."

Chapter 7

As Tempy drove back to Pendleton, her phone buzzed. For safety sake, she answered the phone using her Bluetooth. She was trying to be careful. When the phone rang, her mind was still not on the highway. She was engrossed in thought about the bank books and speculating about how much could be in the accounts; she also wondered why those women reacted the way they did when she said she was related to Adams and Calhoun. Maybe the two bank books contained something special. What could it be?

She answered the phone, saying, "Tempy here, how may I help you?"

"Hello, this is Shawn Mitchell; how are you today?"

"Hi, Shawn. I am fine. What can I do for you this fine afternoon?"

"Tempy, would you like the position here at South Carolina Bank and Trust?"

"Would I? Yes, I sure would."

"Can you come by the bank this afternoon and sign your hiring forms? We want the hiring process wrapped up today, so we can get you started first thing in the morning."

"Yes, I can. I should be there in about thirty minutes. I was on my way back to town, anyway."

She realized someone there could tell her how much these two-bank accounts had in them.

"Shawn, I was wondering if you could look at some documents I found and help me with a problem."

"Well,, Tempy, bring me what you found, and if at all possible, I will help you clear up the mystery."

Tempy arrived at the bank about three thirty. As she walked toward the bank, Shawn was waiting and opened the huge plate glass door for her. As she stepped past him, he handed her the paperwork she needed to fill out to complete the hiring process. She sat down, reached into her handbag, removed the two bank books, and handed them to him.

The printing on the two bank books had long worn off from use and time (they had been created in 1818); she couldn't tell which bank the accounts were from. She was looking for any clue about which bank they came from.

Many years had passed since Tempy's ancestors left the Pendleton area. In the years since they moved on to settle unknown parts of a growing country, no one in her family tried to find any more information about them. She wanted to learn more about what the Genealogical Society found during her visit. She was curious to see where the information they provided her would lead in her family research.

When she got out of bed that morning, she was struggling, but she was about to know a kind of happiness she had never known before. She knew those accounts were important, for the workers to react the way they did when she asked about her two ancestors.

"Shawn, can you tell me how much money is in these accounts today? Are they worth my time placing them into my name? The Genealogical Society in Anderson gave them to me and said they were applying the funds from these accounts to keep up the estates and pay the taxes on them every year.

"Someone even told me about the employees at the society would not let the bank disclose how much was in those accounts today. They thought the value in those account books was none of their business. And with their not knowing, there was less temptation of someone taking money from them."

Shawn looked at the account books, and his eyes grew wide when he saw the names on the. He was shocked; these two men were the largest depositors South Carolina Bank and Trust had. He didn't know how much the accounts contained, but he was well aware it was a substantial amount of money.

He told Tempy the two bank books belonged to South Carolina Bank and Trust; they were from another time. He could still tell they were theirs, or at the least the bank the preceding owner owned. When James purchased the bank, he kept all the accounts owned by patrons of the preceding bank. Previous customers and some of their board members remained with the bank after changing owners.

"Did the ladies at the Genealogical Society ask you to verify your lineage to these two men?" he asked.

"Yes, they did. John Calhoun's father was my seventh great-grandfather. I did one of my Supplements to the Daughters of the American Revolution, using him as my ancestor. They checked my lineage with the DAR, and when they were convinced my history was correct, they handed me these."

"OK, as long as they checked everything out before they gave these to you. When they left Pendleton during the early 1800s, they spelled out that only direct-line descendants could inherit the estate. Genealogical Society staff would pay the taxes out of the accounts until someone came to claim the property and the houses. Let's see what we have here, Tempy. I'm not sure what these accounts are worth today. I'll get someone in here who can get that kind of information off our computers for us."

Shawn opened his door and said, "Brandi, can you come in here and help me figure out what is in these passbooks?"

"Yes, sir, I'll be right there."

She walked into the room and asked, "What can I help you with, Mr. Mitchell?"

"I need you to see if we still carry these two accounts and how much is in them in today's funds."

Brandi looked at the computer screen and told him these were their accounts. She showed him how to find the total in the accounts for himself.

"Mr. Mitchell, I don't have to go do anything; the bank has already recorded these accounts with their sums in our computers. If you enter either of these men's names, you will find what you are looking for. We adjusted these accounts two years ago to reflect today's funds. The head genealogist at the Genealogical Society would not let me put what they would be worth today in them, but we changed our records to show that information for our benefit. Were you aware Mr. Calhoun owned the largest account this bank has?"

"Yes, I knew he was our largest depositor, but how much are we talking about?"

"Almost $2 billion," Brandi said, "with the funds they left in the account and the interest that has accrued over the last one hundred and ninety-seven years."

"What about the account belonging to John Adams?" Shawn asked.

"Sir, there is just shy of $2 billion in that account too. When you told me who we were talking about, I pulled them up before I came in here. These were not ordinary men when they lived here in the Pendleton area. It is my understanding each of them left their overseers this money for their use in keeping up their plantations and their property after they moved. They did not want to sell the property or give it to someone else.

"I understand something happened to both men, and neither one of them ever came back to the area. When their overseers left, after the Civil War, they left the bank books with the Genealogical Society, who has been using the money in these accounts to pay the taxes and keep the properties up since that time."

Tempy overheard the figures Brandi and Shawn were talking about, and the more they talked, the harder it was to concentrate on what she was doing. She could feel the excitement building inside her. She felt like getting up and dancing a jig. She could not believe how fortunate she had become since leaving Jacksonville. Her luck had taken a turn for the better in the brief time she had been away from her hometown.

She could not shake the feeling she had about Tom the afternoon she left him at Beth's. She knew Beth had tried years before to get Tom to divorce her, but Tempy had no way of controlling what went on from over one hundred fifty miles away. Tempy felt like she was in a war zone. Over the last two days, so much good had happened in her life, and she was grateful for whatever or whoever brought her to Pendleton. The last few days were the best thing that ever happened to her. Tempy hoped she could get her life straightened out before someone tried to take it all away.

"As a bonus," Shawn added, "there is a condominium owned by the bank you could live in if you want it. You could stay in the condo or someday find a place of your own."

Brandi turned around and looked at him in surprise. In the eight years she had been with South Carolina Bank and Trust, no one had ever used the condominium. She didn't know this was a benefit of working for James. As far as she knew, no one had used the condo since James bought the bank. Brandi wondered what made Temperance Pierce so special. She said nothing to Shawn about what she had overheard, but she was curious; who was Tempy to get such special treatment from management?

"Instead of living there at the bed and breakfast, you can have a place of your own and get settled a lot quicker. The condominium is in a convenient location, close enough to walk to work when it is nice outside. Would you like to have the condominium?"

"Yes, sir, I would like to have it, for the time being, anyway. I need a place to live, and the condominium seems perfect. Is the condo furnished? And can my dogs live with me?"

"South Carolina Bank and Trust keeps the condominium furnished. Yes, we are pet friendly. It has a fenced-in backyard, which would be perfect for your dogs to run around in the afternoon. Is there anything else you need right now?"

"Yes, sir, I need a car. I drove a U-Haul truck up here and returned it yesterday. I rented a car after my interview yesterday. After I return the car, I'll need a way of getting around."

After Tempy finished the paperwork, she left the bank and headed back to the bed and breakfast. She did not notice James, standing in the doorway of his office, watching her and Shawn. Tempy was ecstatic; everything she had ever wanted was just handed to her by people she had never met before in her life. She did not know how she had gotten so lucky or even how to thank them. She had no intention of wasting a moment of what fate had given her.

Chapter 8

A little over eight years ago, James built himself a great two-story brick home between Pendleton and Columbia. The kitchen was a chef's dream to work in. It had an eight-burner stove, the oven could cook meals at two different temperatures at one time, and he had every conceivable appliance you could want.

James built his house far enough from the main highway to be unseen by people driving by. He enjoyed being tucked away in a wooded area. James purchased the property and had the house built there because it was isolated from the rest of the countryside.

During all this time, he found no one to share his life with. He always kept in the back of his mind that he would bring Tempy to Pendleton somehow, someday. She was always the woman of his dreams, the woman he wanted to grow old with. Tempy and James had been tight when they were young, and he wanted her back in his life.

For seven years, he planned out how to get her to Pendleton. In the last couple of weeks, he put that plan into motion and got her to where he wanted her. He knew now was the time; he was ready for some companionship.

After being alone for so long, he was a little scared of telling someone his secrets. He was more than a little concerned about how she was going to react when she learned he had manipulated her to get her to Pendleton.

He was delighted with how well things were working out at the bank. The first part of his plan went just as he wanted, and to make him even happier, nobody suspected he had anything to do it.

As he had done every afternoon for the last eight years, he hung around the bank until after everyone else left for the day before starting his solitary ride home. He preferred to leave after everyone else because of his dislike of crowds. He became a loner and a selfproclaimed recluse in his eight years in Pendleton. It had been a long time since he showed any emotions for anyone. Sometimes, he wondered if he even liked himself anymore. James declined to get close to people. Few in his circle ever got familiar enough to discuss the past with him. If he felt like talking, he'd say good morning to the bank employees. Women, however, could not get close to him; he wouldn't speak to them, even in passing.

"James, be careful what you say in front of other people," Shawn warned. "You don't want anyone to find out you were friends with Tempy before she came here. It could cause trouble for her with the other employees, and you could have problems with the board of directors."

"OK," he said. "I want her here, but I don't want anyone to think she was hired because I knew her. I pulled the strings to get her to Pendleton. I'll do whatever it takes to make sure she calls Pendleton home. I'm aware I am manipulating her, but I have to."

James thought he got over his feelings for Temperance Brewer long ago. He tried everything he could think of to push her memory out of his mind, but she was still there, just like always. Now he pulled strings to hire her to work under him. Her job in accounting required her to go to board meetings with him once or twice a month, talk to patrons with him, and undertake other business dealings.

He did not get involved with any women since he came to Pendleton. He hadn't had a relationship with a woman since long before he came there. He had to be careful now, or everything he worked for over the last eight years would be in jeopardy. He did not want her to figure out his secret before he was ready.

James knew Tempy before; however, he would let everyone at the bank believe he just met her. He couldn't afford anyone making inquiries into her past. He kept the background information about her to a minimum.

He had many memories of Tempy. He tried to push them aside, but his mind kept wandering back to her. He found his old feelings for her were greater than he had ever imagined. He was finding those feelings were deeper than ever. He tried to keep his feelings for her under control, but he was losing the battle. These old feelings for Tempy returned, and they were as powerful as they ever were. His mother never allowed him to reveal his feelings for Tempy, and he was finding now they were deeper than he had admitted to himself.

James could not help hoping Tempy could deal with the fact once he got up the courage to tell her about himself. For now, however, he had to leave her in the dark about what was going on with him and pray she could handle the truth. He was still scared she would get furious and walk out of his life again. He could not handle that.

When Tempy first met him, he was married to a friend of hers. She told him she wanted more out of life than to be someone's mistress. She knew his wife was at home, pregnant. Tempy wanted to find someone she could love and not have to keep as a secret. Someone she could call her own.

James recalled that many years ago, she always made him feel like he could do anything he put his mind to. Just being in the same room with her made him feel at peace with himself. Seeing her again brought out those same feelings in him. When they shook hands, something happened, and he hoped nobody noticed but him. He never wanted any other women, but now he wanted Tempy. He could not help himself; he hoped she couldn't see how attracted he was to her. He would have to keep his emotions in check and his desires to himself just a little while longer. If he could control himself when she was around, he might make this work. He could have his deepest desire come true.

He wanted to take their relationship slow and get to know who Tempy was today before he tried to take their relationship to another level. He did not want to scare her away when he was so close to getting what he wanted. He could already feel the bond reforming with her, but he thought he should keep his distance from her so she would not find out what was going on.

He told Shawn to make Tempy as comfortable as he could. As far as she knew, the bank was letting her use the condo for as long as she wanted to stay there. No one knew the condo was in James's name and he was letting her use it himself.

James told Shawn to get the condo cleaned and furnished before Tempy arrived. He didn't want her to worry about anything while she settled in her new town. Most of all, he wanted her to find some friends first. More than anything, he wanted to call himself her first true friend there in Pendleton. After they became friends again, he would consider letting her in on his secret.

As James walked through the back door of his house that afternoon, his home phone was ringing. He never turned his cell phone on in his car. He saw the phone as a nuisance he'd rather run from as much as possible. He talked all day on the phone at the bank and didn't like to be bothered after work.

"Jim, we forgot something," Shawn said. "Tempy needs a car."

"Get her one, Shawn," he said. "I meant what I said this afternoon; make sure she has whatever she needs. Do this for me; at least take care of her for the time being. I cannot tell her what's going on yet, but I want her taken care of until I do."

"Are you still going to tell her what's going on with you?"

"I'm not sure if I can go through with our plan. I'm having serious doubts, but I want this woman in my life. I am sure of that much. I am worried about getting too close to her."

"You afraid she might get the wrong idea about you?"

"No, I'm afraid she'll see all the scars on my face and run for the hills before I get close to her again. If I move too fast, I might not get the chance to tell her what happened all those years ago. I'd like to see her; do you think she'd see me tonight?"

"Hold on, Jim; give her time to get settled. She just got here. As far as she knows, you're just her boss. Give her a few days at least; take it slow. You don't want to scare this poor woman to death. We have already manipulated the last three days of her life more than she knows. She might have a problem if we keep interfering in her life. Let's give her a little breathing room and see what happens."

"You're right. I'll get to know her and become a part of her life again. You're also right about the fact she might tell us both to go jump in the lake when she finds out what we have been up to. She never got upset with all the secrets before, but she might not like what we've done to get her to Pendleton. I will leave it at that for now, but you already know what she means to me."

James saw what he had always seen in Tempy, and he wanted what he remembered back. He had to be careful, though, not to reveal too many of the facts of his life to others. But with Tempy, he didn't care what anyone said; he would do whatever it took to get her back into his life. He would try to get to know the person she was now. He was hoping he could find the happiness his and Tempy's parents denied them all those years ago.

Chapter 9

Tempy drove back to the bed and breakfast in Pendleton. As she walked to her room to gather her belongings, she thought about how much her life had changed in two short days. She packed her bags into her rental car, glanced around to take in the magnificent view, and walked back inside to check out. Her heart was happy, and her soul was at ease. For the first time in a long time, she could not wipe the smile off her face. She could not help it, but she felt like she was walking on air.

She headed into town and drove to the condo Shawn had given her the keys to. She was still in an unfamiliar place, alone, but she felt that everything would be all right. She had not felt this good about anything for many years. She was becoming more independent; she liked not having to ask anybody for approval to do anything. She felt comfortable coming and going as she wished and making friends with whoever she wanted.

Tom never allowed Tempy to make new friends, especially men friends. During their years together, if she made friends with another man, Tom would accuse her of cheating on him. He was never reasonable when it came to other men. He could have friends who were women, but men were a threat to him, and he didn't allow anyone to have anything to do with her. He was also jealous of her daughter Lizzie, which made it tough for them to have family dinners. He did not want Lizzie around her mom and made no qualms about how he treated her.

All her life, people kept her isolated, but now she was on her own and could make her own decisions about everything: what friends to choose, where she would live, and where she would work. She no longer needed to make anyone happy but herself.

She parked in the condo's parking lot, walked up to the front door, and turned the key in the lock. It was like a dream. She didn't expect to have a place to call her own so soon. She walked in and looked around her new home. It was the most beautiful place she had ever seen. The condo was bigger than her home back in Jacksonville. She walked into the kitchen and stood there in wonder. The kitchen was bigger than her childhood home's kitchen and living room combined.

Tempy sat down in the living room to watch TV before turning in for the night. After the news finished, she turned it off. After she checked the doors and windows to make sure she locked them, she retired upstairs to bed. The dogs had enjoyed their new yard and the time they got to spend there before bed. They enjoyed it so much she had to tell them more than once that it was time for bed.

Her bedroom had a new king-size bed, and the three poodles took advantage of the extra room. One was sprawled across Tempy's legs, one was lying across her arm, and the other one was lying under the air conditioner vent.

Her alarm clock went off at seven o'clock the next morning. Tempy showered, dressed, and fixed some breakfast; then she took the dogs out back for a walk and was ready to start the new day and face her new life. She might still be alone in a strange town, but she knew she would not be alone much longer.

She looked forward to making friends after living without them for so long; everybody needs at least one friend they can talk to. She wanted to have many friends in her life. She decided to make friends that very first day and didn't care what she had to do to do it.

Before she went the bank that morning, she took the rental car back. Now, she'd have to walk to work, but she was no stranger to walking. Back in Jacksonville, she had bought a car that soon developed problems. Her car needed more repairs than she could afford, so she returned the car to the dealer and walked everywhere she needed to go.

When she got to the bank, Shawn was waiting for her at the door. He showed her to her new office. It was on the second floor at the top of the stairs. She could see everything that happened in the bank from her office door. She could also see James's office windows. She could tell the curtains were closed, and as she walked by his office, she felt sorry that he shut himself off from other people.

Brandi and the other tellers were surprised to see Shawn escorting Tempy up to her office. He never did that before, and they wondered what made her so special. They thought she was receiving special treatment because Shawn liked her, and he didn't bother to say anything to contradict their assumptions.

But to James and Shawn's dismay, employees and customers alike were asking questions. Everyone heard that Tempy was receiving special treatment from Shawn, including the use of the condo, which no one else ever had the pleasure of settling in. Tempy didn't know what others were saying about her. She was enjoying her first day at work and was having a wonderful day.

Part of her responsibilities was to approve or reject projects and loans for the bank. She also had to keep up with the bank's monetary condition. If she noticed anything that would affect the bank's capital, she was to let Shawn and James know. Her other duties included some time traveling with James to the monthly board meeting to present the bank's financial reports.

Shawn helped her get accustomed to her new office and introduced her to the people she'd be working with. She was so overwhelmed that she almost forgot she needed to eat lunch. That is, until her belly reminded her. It was growling, and she wondered if the tellers on the first floor could hear it. While she tried to decide where to go to eat, her phone buzzed, surprising her. Who on earth could be calling her?

Chapter 10

Earlier that morning, Tempy was in one of the stalls in the bathroom when she overheard two women talking about James; one of them suggested he was gay. No one ever saw him with another woman. Tempy thought he was miserable, leading a solitary life. She remembered how being alone as a youngster affected her. She decided to become closer to James and give him at least one new person he could call his friend.

* * * * * *

Evelyn Bohannon, one of the women Tempy overheard in the restroom, was forty-five years old and attractive. She told Brandi she had tried for eight years to get James to notice her, but she could not turn his head. She could not imagine why anyone wouldn't want to be with her. She thought she was the catch of the century and no one else would be good enough for him.

"I was here when he purchased the bank," she said, "and in all that time, I've never known him to speak to a woman."

"I know," Brandi said. "I've been here almost as long as you and cannot remember him being with a woman. What makes Tempy any different? She walked into the bank and turned his head the day she interviewed for the job. I don't understand it."

"What do you mean?"

"When Shawn finished her paperwork yesterday, he gave Tempy the keys to the townhouse the bank has for prominent guests."

"You mean he gave her the townhouse to live in? He's never done that for anybody else before."

"Yes, Tempy's living in the townhouse until she finds a permanent place to live."

"After all these years, she seems to be the one who turned his head."

"I guess, but I was hoping it would be me."

"Yeah, I know what you mean."

Evelyn had hidden her feelings for James, but she was far from delighted with Tempy. She decided to get even with James or make it so no one else would want him.

"Brandy, a little voice in my head whispers to me all the time , If you cannot be with him, then make it where nobody wants anything to do with him."

Neither of the women knew Tempy was listening, and she decided to keep what she heard to herself. It bothered her that any employee would think it was all right to talk about their employer in such a public place.

* * * * * *

James had meetings away from the bank all morning. During these meetings, all he could think about was Tempy. All his thoughts were about seeing her again. He could not get her off his mind, and it distracted him from the business he had to deal with. He decided to ask her out to lunch with him. After his last meeting, he drove back to the bank as fast as he could.

When he got back, he came through the back door so no one would know he had returned. When he got into his office, it was about twelve thirty, and he worried that Tempy had already left for lunch. He needed an excuse to spend time with her, but he didn't want to give anyone reason to suspect anything. He thought lunch was an excellent way to spend a little time with her.

He picked up his phone and dialed Tempy's extension. When she answered, her voice took James back to his younger days, days he missed more than he could ever describe to anybody.

"Tempy, James Braden here," he said after snapping out of his reverie. "Would you like to have lunch with me today, or have you already eaten?"

"No, I haven't eaten," she said. "And I would love to have lunch with you. But James, there are so many other women here who want to go out with you, and they've known you longer than I have."

He had no idea what to say at first, then he answered, "I remember being new in town. I didn't want you to have to eat alone. As for all these other women. I've never gone out with any of them. They know I'd rather not date at this stage in my life, especially not a coworker."

She told him she'd go to lunch with him but wondered why he was changing his policy about dating a coworker. It made her a little suspicious, but she couldn't figure out what was going on.

She wondered why he distanced himself from people that way and vowed to get him to trust her enough to tell her what was going on. James needed friends like everybody else, and she would make certain he thought of her as one of his close friends. She remembered how it felt to have no one to talk to.

To her surprise, she felt a crazy attraction to him, which began that first afternoon when they shook hands. She never had that kind of reaction to anybody before. Well, there had been one other man, but it was long ago. For some reason, she was comfortable around James. She never believed in love at first sight, and she was reluctant to admit she was attracted to him.

She was aware that James was her employer, and that relationship made her feelings for him inappropriate. She knew she was crossing the line, but she did not care. She wanted to make a relationship with him work. She wanted him, and that seemed wrong and right all at the same time. There was something familiar about this man. She had to find out why she was so drawn to him.

She realized employees should not fantasize about their employer, but all she could do was think about him. This was a line she preferred to honor, but whenever she was around him, she found it hard to keep under control. Her fantasies were improper and made her feel dirty every time she had those kinds of thoughts about him.

After hanging up the phone, Tempy walked out of her office and went down the stairs. She met James outside his office, and they headed out the door; she felt as though she was on top of the world. When the other women saw them walk out together, they were amazed; James never went anywhere with anybody other than Shawn Mitchell. Everyone was in complete shock. In the eight years he had been there, no one had ever seen him with a woman, but there he was, going to lunch with Tempy.

Every woman in the bank had the same question: "What's so extraordinary about Tempy? She's only been working here for a few hours, and already she is having lunch with James."

James took Tempy to his favorite Chinese restaurant. Everyone who worked there was surprised when they saw him come in with a woman. He always came in alone or with Shawn; no one had ever seen him with a woman.

James asked to sit in the booth in the back corner. He didn't want anyone to bother them while they had lunch. He had been coming to this restaurant since he moved to Pendleton and realized he might encounter someone he knew in the restaurant, but he wanted privacy today more than ever. He wanted to devote as much time to Tempy as he could, without the fear of intrusion or people trying to figure out what was going on between them.

When the waiter came over to their table, all the poor man could get to come out of his mouth was, "Mr. Jim, you want your regular?"

James always got broccoli beef, hot and sour soup, egg roll, steamed rice, and sweet tea with lemon.

"Yes, please," he said.

"And you, ma'am, what can we get for you?"

"I'd like the Hunan shrimp, Tempy said, continuing, "Steamed rice, hot and sour soup, egg roll, and sweet tea with lemon."

"Yes, ma'am; it will be right out."

"Thank you."

After the waiter left, Tempy began looking through her purse for her cell phone. She had been searching for it all morning. She recalled slipping it into her purse before leaving for work that morning. While she went through her purse, she found the deeds the ladies at the Genealogical Society had given her the day before. She pulled them out of her purse and laid them on the table.

"What do you have there?" James asked.

"I'm not sure," she answered. "I got these documents from the Genealogical Society and stuffed them into my purse yesterday. I forgot about them until now. I may need help figuring out what they are."

"Hand them to me," he said. "I'll look at them for you."

She handed him the papers, and James took great care opening them up. They were so old, he was afraid they might fall apart in his hands if he held them too tightly. He read over one of the deeds, placed it carefully on the table, and sat with his mouth hanging wide open.

After a minute, he leaned over and told Tempy, "This deed is for fifty-five hundred acres of land that belonged to John Calhoun in Oconee County. Tempy, you are the rightful owner of the land, and whatever else is out there is yours as this man's legitimate heir." Tempy could hardly believe what she was hearing James say.

"What about this one?"

"Let's see what it has to tell us."

He read the papers and said, "This deed is for twenty-five hundred acres of land adjoining the first property."

Tempy was stunned; after a few minutes, she gathered her wits and asked him, "Are these deeds for real or is someone pulling my leg? Is someone trying to see how much of a laugh they can get at my expense? James, what about these? The ladies at the Genealogical Society gave me these other papers yesterday. This is the first time I have looked at it."

"This is a deed to the business next door to the bank. An accountant down the street handles the bills and pays its payroll every week. No one in town knows how this agreement worked. This provides you with another source of income beside your position at the bank. You can go over there tomorrow and find out more about their business. After visiting them, you can decide if you want things to continue as they are."

Tempy was even more shocked to hear she owned the business next to the bank. She still thought someone was playing a joke on her and told James that. He looked at her and laughed.

"No, Tempy, they are real. No one is playing a joke on you. If you want, we could drive up to Oconee County this weekend and find out what's up there."

"That sounds good, James."

James never wanted anyone to get too familiar with him. They might see the scars and ask him too many questions, questions he could not answer. But if Tempy could handle the truth, he would not have to answer too many questions. She already knew about him, after spending most of her teenage years with him. He hoped she could handle the truth and would not be too mad about the way he and Shawn had manipulated her to get her to Pendleton.

As they sat and ate their lunch, Tempy enjoyed talking to James. She had not had an ally she could talk to since Taylor Michaels. They often sat in the woods and talked all those years ago. She somehow felt a similar connection to James. When she left Jacksonville and Tom, she decides she needed to find a good friend, someone who loved her for her, not for what they thought she had. She hoped she and James could form that kind of relationship. She knew she had only just met him, but she felt like she had known him forever. She was eager to see where this relationship might take her. She was aware she had feelings for this man and could not wait for their friendship to develop.

Chapter 11

When they were at lunch, Tempy noticed that when someone took out their phone and took some pictures in the restaurant, James had turned away from them. He turned his entire body around, giving no one the chance to get a straightforward shot of his face. She wondered why he did that, but she also wondered why she had feelings of déjà vu every time she spent time with him.

She could not make these feelings go away. She could not shake the feeling she knew him from somewhere else. As her feelings grew stronger, she decided she would find out about his past and figure out this crazy attraction she felt for him every time he got near her. She needed to know why she felt that way.

She and James walked back to the bank. When she went into her office, she saw someone had left four folders on her desk; they were loan applications for her to analyze. As she sat down, she noticed some of her desk drawers were open, as though someone was looking for something.

She knew she could do the job they hired her to do and decided she'd use her education and experience to do the best she could. She wished to be fair with everyone, so she took the first folder and read over the proposal. She thought it was a good idea, but as she plunged into the financials, she saw there was not enough capital to back such a scheme. On the grounds of inadequate funding, she rejected the application.

After she finished, she picked up the second folder and began to read over the application. She thought this also sounded like an excellent idea, and to her delight, she found there was sufficient funding for the proposal. She approved the proposal.

After analyzing those two applications, she glanced at her wristwatch and saw it was after five o'clock; her first day at her new job was over. She sat back in her chair and couldn't believe how quickly the day had gone by. She felt good about the day and got ready to go home.

Before starting the walk home, Tempy decided to go into the office next door and see what they did. She spent about an hour talking with everyone and then left to walk home.

As she began her walk through the parking lot, James was waiting for her.

"I'll see you at the condo around nine o'clock on Saturday," he said.

"Really?" she asked.

"Yes, we can drive out to the Adams and Calhoun estate in my car."

"Oh, that's right. Thanks."

She had forgotten all about James offering to go with her to Oconee County. She thought he was just being nice to a new employee, but she was happy he offered to go with her. After taking her rental car back, she had no way to get out there.

Tempy walked home and went into the condo; she changed her clothes and went outside with her three poodles to enjoy the afternoon. After they came back in, she fixed herself some dinner and settle back to enjoy a little TV. As she watched the evening news, she could not get over how peaceful it was to be there.

A little after eight o'clock, there was a knock at Tempy's door. She couldn't imagine who it could be. No one knew she was in Pendleton. She answered the door and saw James standing in her doorway. He smiled and asked if he could come in for a little while. Tempy was confused but welcomed him into her home. She hoped the shock she felt seeing him there did not show on her face. She tried to act as natural as she could, but her stomach felt far from normal.

After she invited James to sit down, she asked if he would like a drink.

"Yes," he said, "a glass of sweet tea would be nice."

"OK, I'll be right back. My dogs will keep you company until I get back."

"OK."

She went into the kitchen and fixed him a glass of tea. She brought it to him, and he drank it while they watched TV and chatted. As he finished, they kept talking. James wanted them to get to know each other a little better.

They talked until about eleven o'clock that night. As James got up to leave, his hand brushed against hers. Their eyes met, and they both backed away from one another. Something was developing between them, but Tempy could not figure out why she was so fascinated with him. She knew something was different about him; she would have preferred getting to know someone before having them over to her home. But there was something about James, she could not get a handle on. She needed to get her feelings for him in check, though. She needed to remember; he was her employer.

He turned to go, and she walked him to the door. As he opened the door, he turned and kissed her softly on her cheek. Tempy wanted more, but she decided to take this slow and easy.

"Tempy, Shawn's my only friend," he said. "I want another friend, and I'd like that to be you."

"I would love that, James."

"That's good, Tempy, and thank you."

"For what?"

"For sitting and talking without wanting something from me. I may never be able to give myself to anybody again. There are women at the bank who want to be with me, but I don't want them in that manner. I cannot see myself with a woman at this point in my life. I don't think

I am ready for that just yet. If you can wait for me to figure out how to be with people again, I'd like to get closer to you."

"You're welcome, James; you've kept yourself away from other people for so long, you forgot how to be you. I'll be whatever kind of friend you need. There is something about you that is so familiar, and I like the way you make me feel about myself and life."

"Sounds like you are speaking from experience."

"I am. When I was younger, things happened in my childhood I had to get over, and it took me a long time. After many years of therapy, I moved past my childhood. Things happened that made me doubt my self-worth and question what people wanted from me. I had to take a while after high school to figure out who I was. I loved who I was turning into, and I want to find her again."

"I will see you tomorrow at the bank."

"Yes, you will."

After James left, she let the dogs out back and went to bed after they came back in. She could not get the feel of James's touch and kiss out of her mind. She fell asleep with a smile on her face, and she felt even more content when she woke up the next morning. After getting out of bed, she took a few minutes to sit on the deck while the dogs played outside. When they finished, she put them in the house, picked up her purse, and began walking to the bank.

As she approached the bank, she saw a brand-new car sitting outside the front entrance; it was a Ford Mustang GT. She stepped inside and started up the stairs to her office. Shawn called her back downstairs and handed her a set of keys.

"What are these?" she asked.

"The keys to your new Mustang out front. It belongs to you."

"Really? What did I do to get to be so special?"

"We don't want you to have to walk to work if it rains, so we decided since you don't have a car, we'd get you one."

"We, meaning you and James?"

"Yes, that's right."

"Thank you; that's so nice of you."

"Enjoy it, Tempy."

She looked around the corner to see if James was in his office, but he was not there yet. Just then, she saw him come in the door and head into his office. She walked over and knocked on his door.

"James, can I talk with you for a minute?" she asked as she went into his office.

"Sure," he said. "What's up?"

"Well, let me see. What is this? I didn't mean for you to get me a car."

"You need one. You can tell everybody you had the dealer deliver it to the bank."

"OK, but that is a lot for a gift. What's going on?"

"I don't want you walking to and from work, especially in the rain."

"OK, next thing: Did I do something last night that was improper?"

"No, why do you ask?"

"Well, you are my boss and getting too familiar with you is not appropriate."

"I know, but sometimes we have to ignore the rules and live our lives the way we want to. Besides, this is a family-owned business, and I want you to feel like my family."

"I want to ask you something, but I don't want you to run from me like you do everybody else."

"OK, what do you want to know?"

"Why me, and why now? You haven't dated a woman in over eight years. I only met you three days ago, but I find myself attracted to you. I don't know what it is, but there's something familiar about you. I don't want to do something that might cause you to hide from me like you do the other women here."

"Tempy, I'm flattered that you care more about my feelings than your own."

"I am, and I don't want you to assume I am trying to throw myself at you or force you into doing something you do not want to do."

"I won't. See you in a little while."

"OK, have a great day."

As Tempy turned to walk away from James, he stopped her and kissed the back of her hand. Something about his touch sent chills all over her. She was falling in love with him, but for the life of her, she could not figure out why. She had not known him long enough for any kind of attachment to form.

As she walked back to her office, she thought, *Why are James and Shawn being so nice to me? What did I do to deserve all this special treatment from them?*

Chapter 12

On Saturday morning, Tempy got up, took a shower, and got dressed. She planned to wear something suitable for hiking in the woods. She had not been hiking since she was a girl. She found a pair of blue jeans, a short-sleeve shirt, and a light jacket. Her jacket would warm her arms if it got cooler in the woods in Oconee County.

James made it to Tempy's condo a little after nine o'clock. He wore an old pair of jeans and a tee shirt; she could see every muscle on his chest. She let him in, and he waited for her in the living room while she finished getting ready.

When she walked down the stairs into the living room, James was struck by how beautiful she looked in a pair of jeans. She reminded him of the girl he had known all those years ago.

He took a few minutes to regain his composure and then asked, "Are you ready for a day in the woods with me?"

James felt his face and cheeks turning red and hoped she didn't notice; he needed this woman in his life again so much, he didn't know what to do. With Tempy standing in front of him, he wanted to reveal the truth about himself.

Just then, Tempy's doorbell rang, and she turned around to answer it.

James wanted this woman so much, it hurt for him to breathe. Every fiber of his being needed to touch her and be with her. He found being alone with her made it hard to contain himself. He wasn't sure how long he could control his desires at this rate.

Tempy opened the door, and there stood Shawn. He also wore clothing fit for a day in the woods. She invited him inside before they drove out to the property. James was glad to see Shawn there. The doorbell had allowed him a chance to get his lustful feelings under control.

Tempy had not noticed James's reaction to her. She still had to take care of the dogs before she left them for the day. It would be a few hours before she came back, and she needed to make sure they had enough food and water.

"Well, I can't wait to spend a day in the woods with you. This is like being a teenager again back home in Jacksonville. It will give me the opportunity to do something I've always loved doing."

"What's that, Tempy?" Shawn asked.

"When I was growing up, I went for hikes in the woods behind my house. I could remain in those woods for hours and never miss the world that was turning just on the other side of the tree line."

"What did you like about it?"

"It was quiet there, and I could think. I couldn't have friends when I was a teenager. My parents were afraid I might see my former boyfriend again, and they could not have that. So they made every parent in the neighborhood mad at them, so they could separate me until I was eighteen."

"Did it work?"

"As far as they knew."

James was so taken with how Tempy looked in an old pair of jeans and a tee shirt, he stumbled for words to express himself. His thoughts were so far away, he didn't hear Tempy and Shawn chatting.

James needed to come to terms with the woman Tempy had become, and driving with her in his car to the land the Genealogical Society gave her was a good opportunity. He was so engrossed in his own thoughts that he didn't hear Tempy ask him if he was ready to leave. She asked him again, and he still didn't hear a word she said.

Finally,, she grabbed his arm and shook him slightly while saying, "James, are you ready to leave? Where did you go?"

"Yeah, I am. Just remembering my life before I showed up in Pendleton." As he headed toward the door, James knew he would go anywhere Tempy wanted him to go with her.

James found the more time he spent with Tempy, the more he loved her. As the three of them walked to James's car, they chatted about what they might encounter out at the property. As Tempy got into James's car, Shawn told them he would drive by himself and meet them out at the property.

After Tempy got in the car and shut the door, Shawn asked James if he would be OK being so close to her. He reassured him he was fine. He admitted he was having problems keeping his hands under control, but he thought he'd be OK with her.

"Is it becoming that hard to be around Tempy again?"

"Yeah, but you and I know this is a complication I made myself. Now I am getting what I asked for."

"You need to tell her the truth."

"Yes, but I don't want her furious at me. I don't think I could deal with it if she never spoke to me again."

"I'll go along with whatever decision you make."

He had wanted to spend time with Tempy alone. Well now, he was going to get his wish. Well, they would be almost alone; Shawn would be there with if either of them needed anything.

James and Tempy had already spent a pleasant evening together, just visiting. No one was any the wiser about their evening together, and he preferred to keep it that way. He hadn't even told Shawn about his trip to Tempy's the other night.

James thought after spending an evening with Tempy, the tension between them would have lessened, but it had not. Now, they would spend an hour and a half driving to her new property in Oconee County, and then they'd be out in the woods together. James needed to be mindful of what he yearned for; he might slip up and get it. It would not take much prompting for him to blurt out his secret to her. He was finding it more and more difficult to keep his secret between just him and Shawn.

After the long drive to Oconee County, they pulled into the property, and James parked the car to one side. They chatted a few minutes, and when they stepped out of the car, they could see nothing around them but brush. Nothing but woods, bramble briars, and kudzu as far as the eye could see. James could tell it was a marvelous piece of property, and Tempy could imagine building a home here. She knew she was searching for a place she could call her own, and this looked like the ideal spot. There was a view of the Oconee River, the neighboring mountains, and a charming meadow just up on the hillside. Tempy decided it was the ideal spot for her to start over and begin her life. She always had a picture in her head of the place she wanted to move and start her life over again. Her property in Oconee County was what she had dreamed of for the last couple of years.

While she and James were looking around, a car drove up and parked, and an older gentleman stepped out of his car. Before she left that morning, she had called the society to request someone meet them at the property to show them around.

"Hello," the man said. "Do you wish to visit the mansion?"

Tempy looked at him with excitement in her eyes and asked, "There's a house around here?"

"Yes, ma'am, there sure is. Come with me, and I'll show it to you."

Sure enough, not far into the brush, there was an old wooden house. Tempy had learned that John Adams built the house for himself and his first wife, but after she passed away, she left him with the house and the responsibility of taking care of his infant son alone. He was struggling to make a life for himself and his son on this land while he tried to find a new wife.

John found another woman to spend his life with, and he married her four years later. When he did, he took his bride to live with him and his son in that two-room wooden house until they had children of their own, and then they moved to Georgia. This compact house had a kitchen and a living room on one side, but Tempy thought those two rooms would have made three rooms in her home back in Jacksonville. Houses built in those days often had a wide-open walkway built in the center of the house. There were no sides on the walkthrough, so the elements would have moved right through the house winter and summer. She could imagine it was a hard way to live, but she enjoyed seeing how life had been for her ancestors. On the other side of the walkway was the one bedroom where everyone in the family slept at night. Tempy could not believe her family began in this tiny house here in the Oconee County woods, but here she was. She had been doing her family's genealogy for years and knew how many people wound up living in this tiny house. She could feel her ancestors all around her as she stood inside their house.

While she stood inside the house, it felt like someone put their arm around her and whispered, "Everything will be OK; you are home."

As Tempy wandered through the house, she noticed James was limping as he walked around; he held his left leg as if he hurt it earlier in his life. She also noticed that when he walked, he had this cocky attitude about him. It was something she saw before in someone else. While she stood there, she realized where she recognized James from. She realized what it was about him that was so familiar, or so she thought.

James limped and carried himself like her old friend Taylor Michaels had. She barely choked back her emotions as she realized she thought James was Taylor. She wanted to be alone with him when she confronted him with her suspicions. If she was correct, she didn't want anyone else around. She realized this situation would require a gentle touch. James said he purchased the bank because he was tired of his old life and wanted a fresh start. Walking like Taylor could be a coincidence, but she hoped not. She missed him so much and found it hard to think of him without crying like a baby.

As they walked around the property a little longer, Tempy pretended to slow down so she could watch him walk. Every so often, she could see the cocky attitude Taylor used to walk with. She watched for a while, and sure enough, he did it again. He had surgery on his left knee when he was a freshman in high school.

Tempy realized if she was correct about him, he had an excellent reason for keeping his identity a secret. James had worked hard to cover up the truth about himself. But whoever caused this to happen overlooked one crucial thing: the way he walked. He always had a distinctive way of walking, and there it happened again right in front of her. She noticed it three times that morning while they walked through the brush and now again at the house.

Tempy thought she would explode with joy. She could not get the impression out of her head and hoped she was right about this. If true, it explained everything she saw and felt the last week there in Pendleton. She discovered her friend, and she would confront him with what she believed.

When she was ready, Tempy called out, "Taylor!"

James did not stop, but he couldn't believe what she said. He realized she figured it out for herself, but he could not let on to her she was correct. He kept walking and hoped she would figure she mistook him for someone else and let it go. He was not ready to discuss what he knew deep down was coming. He wanted to have this conversation on his time, not hers. He was still not sure he was ready for her to shout at him for the misery he had put her and his entire family through. He knew he had put them through a lot, but things in his life couldn't be avoided.

Tempy felt a pang of uncertainty go through her. Could she have been wrong? He did not want to hurt her, but he was not ready to have that discussion. He pretended not to recognize the name and hoped Tempy would think she was wrong about him.

Tempy was disappointed when he pretended she was mistaken about who he used to be. He just kept walking and hoped he had persuaded her that she was wrong about him. These two men walking alike was just a coincidence. She could not believe how disheartened she was. At that point, she did not wish him to see her break down.

She did, however, recognize who he was. Tempy would give him the time and space he needed and not press him for answers to any of her questions. She did not realize how she knew for certain he was Taylor Michaels, but she did. Something about him not telling her spoke volumes to her. Tempy had seen him close people out all of her life, so she felt as though she had expected him to do his best to persuade her he was not who she thought.

To hide her feelings, she got up and walked around the property by herself. She wanted to make sure she could do what she wanted with the land. If there would be any problems building her home there, she needed to know. She would be happy there with whoever she found to spend the rest of her life with; even if James weren't Taylor, she wanted to get to know him better. There was still something about him that made her feel like she hadn't felt about anyone in a long time. She liked who she was when she was with him and getting to know him seemed like a pleasurable endeavor. She didn't care who he was; she found herself drawn to him. She liked the way he made her feel about herself as a woman whenever he was around.

Chapter 13

James never wanted to hurt Tempy. He knew he shouldn't deny her the satisfaction of knowing who he was, but he wasn't ready for her to know who he was. He never imagined she would guess who he was from the way he walked and carried himself in the woods. As they continued to walk around the land, he asked Tempy if she wanted to drive up to the estate that belonged to John Calhoun. She said yes, but he could tell she was disappointed he did not acknowledge that he was Taylor Michaels.

She began to cry as they walked back to James's car and drove up to the land belonging to John Calhoun. After they drove into the land and parked, Tempy sat in the car for a few minutes to compose herself before going into the Calhoun mansion. James got out and walked around to open the car door for her. He noticed she had been crying while they rode up to the house. She had hoped he wouldn't see her crying. She wanted her friend and lover back. If he wanted to keep his identity from her and everyone else, she could respect his wishes.

"Tempy, are you all, right?" he asked.

"I'm OK. I'll be honest with you: I wanted my old friend back so much, I convinced myself you were him. I was disappointed when I figured out I was mistaken."

James realized he might be wrong about how she'd react to his secret. She might accept it, and they might move forward the way he wanted when he brought her to Pendleton.

As they neared the old antebellum home, Tempy noticed the mansion was still untouched. The mansion was old, but the Genealogical Society brought it into the twenty-first century with plumbing, electric lights, and even an internet hookup. The mansion looked amazing, both inside and out. She thought the residence would be in decay. She did not wish to live in the enormous plantation house, but she felt as though she were at home, standing there at the foot of those beautiful stairs.

Out of nowhere, she felt those comforting arms around her again and could have sworn she heard a woman's voice say to her, "Welcome home, my grandchild."

As James watched Tempy walk around the old house, he wondered what she was feeling. He felt bad he did not reveal the truth to Tempy about himself, but he could not find the courage to admit to her he was Taylor. Not yet; too much had taken place, and he did not feel he was in a good position where his past was concerned. He knew he would have to tell her soon. She would learn the facts if she could just wait until he was ready to tell her.

James did not know Tempy's true feelings for him. She would have wanted to hear his side of the story; she would have welcomed finding her old friend, the one person she wanted back in her life more than anything. She felt lost without him, and now she was having to handle the sadness of losing him all over again. This time was different, though; she would feel the loss in her heart. She wanted to get done at the estate, go home, curl up in a ball, and cry herself to sleep. Her heart was breaking, and she didn't want anyone to know just how much she hurt inside.

As they walked around the estate together, they chatted about her plans for the old antebellum house.

"I have some ideas, but I need to figure out the details before I plunge into anything."

"Will you let me be a part of whatever you develop out here?"

"If that's what you want, I'd love to have you as my business partner."

James knew they had just found the ideal way to spend more time with each other, and no one at the bank would suspect something was happening between him and Tempy. He could not believe his stroke of good luck.

As they walked back to his car, she asked him, "You ready to go back to Pendleton?"

"Yes, but I don't want to go home when we get back."

"You want to stick around and talk for a while?"

"Sure."

"OK."

As James drove back to Pendleton, he glimpsed over at Tempy. She was crying again. He knew he hurt her but he never planned to. He felt so bad about the way she reacted when he didn't tell her the truth. Tempy's reaction made it almost impossible for him to control his feelings and to keep them in check.

When he got to the townhouse, he walked Tempy to her door.

"Tempy, I changed my mind; I'm going home."

"Why? What did I do? I thought you wanted to spend time with me."

"Oh, God. You did nothing wrong. I want to spend more time with you, but I think it's better if we say goodnight now, instead of waiting until later."

"OK, James, I will see you Monday at the bank."

"Yes, you will."

It took all the strength he could muster up not to tell her he loved her. He loved her for as long as he could remember. He knew should reveal his feelings for her, but he wasn't ready for anyone to know his secret. It saddened him to cause her so much grief, but he knew it would only be for a little while longer. He never considered that she might still have feelings for Taylor Michaels. James didn't know his family never gave Tempy the freedom to deal with his death. On the drive back to Pendleton, Tempy decided to go along with what he wanted, for the time being. To her, it was enough that she was knew who he was. She did not want to push him away before she had the chance to gain his trust.

Chapter 14

Tempy spent Sunday alone, struggling to figure out what she wanted most from her life. After yesterday, she realized she needed someone in her life who made her feel special. Her first order of business was to get a divorce from Tom. She also realized she wanted to start over with someone who made her feel like James made her feel. Those things had been missing from her life with Tom for a long time.

Tempy finally saw that all Tom wanted was what he could take from her and maybe a free piece of ass whenever he was in the mood. She realized what Tom had been up to. She told several people over the years she thought he only wanted her for what he thought she might have one day. She didn't want to think of herself as someone else's whore ever again. She wanted to discover herself and then find someone special to spend the rest of her life with, someone who wanted to be with her and wanted to grow old with her.

After she arrived at work on Monday morning, Tempy decided to call Tom to see what he wanted to do about them. Did he want to move to Pendleton and be with her, or did he want to remain in Manchester with Beth and her kids? To Tempy's dismay, Beth answered Tom's phone.

"Tom doesn't want to talk to you ever again," Beth said. "He decided he wants to get a divorce. His lawyer will deliver the papers to you by the end of the week, if you tell us where you are living."

"Beth, you mean it only took you one week to persuade him to divorce me?"

"Yes, his lawyer called it abandonment."

"I asked him if he wanted to move with me. He said he'd rather stay with you until I found a place to live."

"He told his attorney Friday you were cheating on him, bringing men to the house while he waited in the kitchen. His story paints you like the tramp we've always known you to be."

"What does he want from me?"

"A forwarding address so we can send the papers."

"I'll call you later with that information."

Tempy hung the phone up and slid down into her leather chair. Her heart was heavy; Tom's accusation was like a slap in the face. She decided to take care of this situation on her own. She only had two friends in Pendleton, so she went to ask them for help.

She began to cry as she walked downstairs to see if James or Shawn were in their offices. She needed someone to talk to and had no idea where else to turn. Even though James continued to hide his identity, she found herself drawn to him more than anyone she had ever known. She knocked on his door, and when he saw who it was, he invited her into his office. She almost didn't hear him when he told her to come in. She was crying so hard, she couldn't hear anything over her tears.

James looked up from his desk when Tempy walked in and wished her a good morning. She never answered him. He feared she was upset about what happened on Saturday. He got up out of his chair, walked over to where Tempy was standing, and led her to one of the brown chairs in front of his desk. As he pulled the other chair closer to hers, she looked at him with tears streaming down her face and asked, "Do you know any divorce attorneys?"

"Yes, Tempy, I do."

"Would you give me his number? I don't know who else to ask for advice. I need help with a few legal problems."

"Yes, anything, if it will make you stop crying. I cannot stand to see you this upset. Will you tell me what happened?"

"I called Tom a few minutes ago, and his sister told me he filed for divorce."

"Tempy, whatever he is asking for, we can deal with it. Don't worry, it will be OK."

"Yeah, but I don't want anyone here to think what he is accusing me of is true. I feel like I did back in high school. It hurts to think I am being accused of doing things I never did. My life seems to replay the same mistakes over and over. Everyone thinks since I put up with being talked about like that as a kid, I will sit by and let them do the same thing now."

"Tempy, no one here will ever think those rumors were true."

"He told a lawyer I had men in the house having sex with them while he waited in the kitchen. His sister called me a tramp. Right now, I feel dirty. I loathe myself so much, all I want to do is run away and hide and never come out again."

"No one here will ever think they are telling the truth. Shawn and I have been with you every day for the last week and saw no evidence of what he has accused you of."

"But some people might think they are true. No one here knows me."

"You and I have begun to become friends over the last week, and I've seen nothing like anything they are accusing you of."

"James, I need the name of that attorney."

"I'll call him for you and make you an appointment."

"Thank you."

"Tempy, are you mad at me?"

"No, for what? Things in my past are causing this situation with Tom to be almost more than I can stand. I want it to be over with him. They accused me as an adolescent of telling everyone that the guy I loved had raped me. I wanted to climb into a hole then and drag the dirt in on top of me, and now Tom is accusing me of cheating on him with a lot of men while he watched. I feel filthy, like I did as a teenager."

"I am so sorry. I wish …"

"You wish what?"

"That I could comfort you more and make what took place in your past go away."

Tempy leaned over and hugged James. He wanted to pull her closer to him and kiss her to make all her problems go away. He realized, though, if he did, she would recognize him for sure. It saddened his heart she was being made to suffer like she did back in high school. He realized the emotions she was experiencing were hard to handle; some were because of him, but he still could not tell her. He was afraid she would figure out who he was before he was ready. James decided, however, he would support her as best he could without exposing his identity to her.

As Tempy hugged him, he whispered to her, "You are welcome."

Just then, his lawyer, Barry, answered the phone. James told him about Tempy's situation and made an appointment for her for eleven o'clock that morning. Barry made room for her in his schedule and said he'd come by the bank and talk to Tempy because she was friends with James. Barry was a little surprised to find out James was developing feelings for a woman he had only met a week ago.

"Thank you, Barry. I'll see you later."

After he hung up the phone, James helped Tempy back to her office. She was getting more upset by the minute. She never dreamed Tom would lie about her this way, just to get what he wanted from her. She had nothing left to offer him; she felt like she had given him enough. In fact, she already gave him too much of her life and the things she loved in her life. She wanted to crawl into a hole and die. She had no friends and no family to turn to; she was alone, she thought.

James stayed with Tempy until Barry arrived at her office. As Barry walked in, James walked up to him and said, "Let me know before you leave. I don't want her alone in this office."

"You got it, my friend."

Barry did not understand James's fascination with Tempy, but he would do whatever he could to help his friend. He walked over to Tempy's chair and said, "Hello, Tempy. What can I do for you today?"

"I need help with a divorce. My husband, Tom, is accusing me of every dirty thing a person can think of. He's also accusing me of abandoning him when I came to Pendleton a week ago searching for work."

"Who's his lawyer?"

"Antoinette Corolla."

"Is any of what he is saying true?"

"No, I've always been faithful to him, whether I wanted to or not. The only man I wanted died years ago. No one else comes close to him. Will you help me?"

"Yes, for two reasons: First, I deplore the fact you are being painted as an awful person. Second, you found a house and called him to find out if he wanted to rejoin you. I detest it when people try to make a person into someone bad when they are trying to better themselves."

"Thank you, I need the help."

"Do you have Ms. Corolla's phone number?"

Tempy wrote the number down on a piece of paper and gave it to Barry. She got the coloring back into her cheeks as she pulled herself together and quit crying.

"Barry, what do I need to do until this divorce is final?"

"No running around with wild men."

"You can count on that. I don't know anyone here except James and Shawn, and they're not exactly wild men."

"Good. Now, Tempy, I have to ask you a question."

"What's that?"

"If he asks for financial compensation, can you pay it?"

"I can, but the money isn't in my name yet; I don't want him to have access to it since I didn't get it until after I arrived here in Pendleton."

"You think James would loan you any money?"

"I have no idea. I haven't even gotten my first paycheck yet."

"Can we ask him?"

"We can, I suppose."

Tempy picked up the phone receiver and called James's office.

"Can you come back to my office for a minute?" she asked.

"Sure," he said. "I'll be right there."

Tempy and Barry chatted while they waited for James to come upstairs. After he walked into the room, Barry filled him in on what was going on.

"James, are you able to lend Tempy money? She may need a considerable amount of cash."

"Sure, I can run it through the bank as a loan to myself. I know she has the capital from an inheritance, but I think she's given this man enough."

"I agree, but she may need it to finalize the divorce. I'd be glad to help her through this ordeal. I'll call you two when I hear back his lawyer. Take it easy, Tempy; we will fix this."

"Thank you, Barry."

"You are most welcome. Lunch tomorrow, James?"

"Yeah, that will be good. Same place?"

"Sure, I love getting my Chinese fix at that place."

"Me too. I'll call you in the morning to confirm."

Barry left Tempy's office, and James got up to go back downstairs. Before he could get to the door, Tempy stopped him and asked him to wait. He walked back over to the chair next to Tempy's window.

"Could you stay with me for a few more minutes?" she asked. "I don't want to be alone just yet."

"Do we have to stay in the office?" he asked. "I'm starving. You want to go get some lunch with me?"

"Yes, where are we going?"

"I was thinking we might have Mexican today."

"I love good Mexican food."

"I know just the place; you will love it."

"I'm ready when you are."

"Great. You realize the other women in this bank will talk if we keep this up."

"So let them talk. Might do them some good."

"What's going on, Tempy?"

"I told a little lie to Barry. He asked if I've been faithful to Tom, and I have, but when I got to Pendleton, I met someone I want to get to know better, but he doesn't like people getting too close to him. I want him to know I don't care what he did in his past. I want to know the person he is now."

"Are you talking about me?"

"Yes, James. After all the awful things Tom said about me, I wouldn't blame you if you walked out that door and didn't have anything else to do with me. I think since today is the day for the truth, I better tell you the truth: I want to become a bigger part of your life, if you will let me. I want to be your friend, if nothing else. So if the other women in the bank want to talk, let them. You need friends, just like everyone else."

"I would love that, Tempy."

"I'll see you when you get back from your meeting."

"OK, that gives me something to look forward to."

James turned to walk towards the door; Tempy stood up and hugged him. As he walked down the stairs and went back into his office, he thought he was ready to let Tempy back into his life. He wasn't sure where this relationship would wind up, but for the first time in years, he wanted a woman to spend time with him. He brought this woman to Pendleton a week before; now he wanted to let her back into his life. If it was only a little at a time, it was a good start, and he found that some time with Temperance Brewer was better than none.

Over lunch, James told Tempy he had to go to Columbia to meet with the governor and would be away for a couple weeks. He worried about her being in Pendleton alone, with no one to talk to, but he couldn't get out of it; meeting with the governor was important. He gave Tempy his personal phone number so she could call him if she wanted to. He wanted to take her in his arms and make sure she would be all right before he went anywhere.

"Shawn will be around if you need someone to talk to."

"Thank you for trying to take care of me."

"Tempy, you did nothing wrong. The more you listen to what others say about you, the more power you give them over you."

"I feel dirty. Are you sure you want to be near me? I felt this way one other time in my life, back when I was a teenager, and I didn't like the way it made me feel, either."

He thought to himself, Yeah, *I remember those awful years.*

"James, I mean it, thank you for caring about my feelings."

"I care, Tempy. More than you know."

They finished lunch and walked back to James's car. As they drove back to the bank, he held her hand and tried to calm her down. As they drove into the parking lot, he slipped the key to his house into her hand. James asked her to take care of his house while he was gone, and he was sure now that he wanted her to be more than just a friend.

Back inside the bank, he went into his office to collect the paperwork he needed for his meeting with the governor. He told Brandi to cancel his meetings the rest of the week and call Barry to cancel lunch the next day.

Before going home to pack, James called Tempy's office one last time to make sure she was all right. After realizing he had left her in excellent hands, he drove home to pack. He knew she would be OK until he got back; Shawn would see to it.

Chapter 15

James called Tempy every day while he was away. It had been several weeks since he had gone to Columbia, South Carolina, to work on the governor's team to bring more tourists and businesses to the state. He planned to be away for only two weeks, but it turned into six of the longest weeks of his life. He wanted to see Tempy and missed her more than he could ever imagine. At the end of each long day of meetings, he would call Tempy and talk to her for a while.

He was excited about the plans he and the governor were coming up with concerning the economic development in the Pendleton area. Revenue from the new businesses and tourist attractions would mean a great deal to the town, and his involvement would mean a lot to the bank. The fact that the governor had asked him to work on the project was a significant feather in his cap.

Over those six weeks, Tempy enjoyed talking to James every day, but it was not enough. She wanted him back home so she could see him during the day and maybe steal a night here and there for them to be together. No one needed to know they saw each other socially; it was nobody's business but theirs.

When the six weeks were up and James was getting ready to return to Pendleton, he called her and said, "Tempy, can we have dinner tomorrow night at your condo?"

"Sure, James. What's up?"

"I'm coming home tomorrow and will tell you about it then." That afternoon, Barry called to let her know the divorce papers were final and she could come pick them up.

"That was fast," she said. "No arguing, no negotiation?"

"Well,, I think they already spoke to the judge and were waiting to see if we had a counterproposal. It's over, Tempy. You're no longer married to Tom Pierce."

"Thanks, Barry."

"You are most welcome. Have you heard from James?"

"Yes, he's coming back tomorrow night."

"You know you have to wait sixty days before you can get remarried?"

"Yes, I know, but I don't see that happening soon. First, someone must be around long enough to spend time with me to get to that point in a relationship. So far, the only man I'm interested in doesn't have time to spend with me."

Barry could tell she was referring to James. He knew he had been in Columbia for the past month and a half, and the meetings with the governor took all of his time.

During her lunch hour, Tempy went over to Barry's office and came out with the divorce papers in her hand. She was surprised it was over in six weeks, but she was holding the paperwork. As she walked back towards the bank, she could think of nothing else, but the divorce and her plans for the evening with James.

She was moving on with her life, and for the first time in a long time, she was moving in the direction she wanted to go. She could make all her dreams come true. She no longer worried about somebody taking away what belonged to her. She was free to live her life the way she wanted to, make her own mistakes and become the person she wanted to be and be proud of her accomplishments for herself. She would never depend on someone else for approval and self-worth again.

She decided to do whatever it took to make her dreams come true. She was ready for the changes she knew were sure to come and welcomed the new life she was sure to find, no matter who she spent the rest of her life with.

The next morning, she began going through the phone book, looking for contractors to build her dream house. She had been impressed with the bed and breakfast she stayed at those first two nights in Pendleton and wanted to transform the manor house into a bed and breakfast. She had the means to turn the property into a five-star resort in the Oconee woods.

As she was looking through the phone book, her phone rang. It was James; she was overjoyed to hear his voice.

"How are you?" she asked. "Will I see you tonight?"

"I am fine. I'll see you at your place for dinner."

"Do you want me to cook?"

"No, I arranged for a chef to come and fix dinner for us while we spend time together. I do not want you doing anything tonight; I want you to myself. I've been away so long and need to spend time with you. We can talk to each other without worrying about somebody seeing us together."

"OK."

"I'll be there about six o'clock."

"OK, I'll be waiting for you. I have a question: Do you know a good contractor in this area?"

"Yeah, Rick Weber. Tell him I told you to call him. You going to do something with your property?"

"I am. I'll tell you all about it tonight."

"OK; did something else happen?"

"Yes, but I want to wait and tell you about it when you get here tonight. See you then."

"Bye."

"Bye."

After hanging up the phone, Tempy found the number for Rick Weber Construction and called it; a young woman answered and said that Rick would be right with her. Tempy was happy to be moving forward with her new life. She almost had everything she wanted. She could build her dream home and start her own business. The only thing she needed now was for James to get over his fear of people getting too close to him. Since she came to Pendleton, she had broken through some of his defenses. She was sure she had made headway into his life. She believed he was worth the effort, and she would keep trying to get through to him.

When Rick came on the phone, Tempy told him about her property and asked when he could meet her in Oconee County.

"I have some time this afternoon," Rick said. "I'd be happy to meet you in Oconee County to hear what you have in mind for the property."

She had been giving a lot of thought to what she wanted and who she wanted to spend the rest of her life with. If James wanted to be a part of her life, that would be up to him; she would not beg him for his attention. She was moving on with her life and making her own plans.

Tempy drove out to the property and met with Rick around two. He was interested in what she wanted to build out there and was impressed by the amount of thought she had given to the project. As they walked around, she described her plans for the house and grounds. Rick knew the finished project would be beautiful.

After Tempy shared her vision for the property with Rick, she drove him over to the Calhoun estate. Rick stepped out of Tempy's car and was impressed by the old plantation house. No one could believe the good condition it was still in. She was lucky General Sherman did not burn the house to the ground as he marched through the south, burning everything in his path.

Tempy finished showing Rick the two properties and describing her vision of how she saw them when she finished. By this time, it was already three thirty. Rick assured her he could do the project and would have his staff draw up a set of drawings for her to approve so he could get to work on the project in the next couple weeks. He suggested that in the meantime, she could clear up the brush and debris around the old house. He thought the plantation manor house would only need a little remodeling here and there to turn it into a bed and breakfast.

She got back to Pendleton about five thirty, just before James was scheduled to arrive for dinner. She went upstairs to shower and wash the dirt off from walking around the properties. The doorbell rang as she got out of the shower; it was the chef James hired. As tired as she was that afternoon, she was glad he arranged for someone to cook.

James arrived at Tempy's condo about six thirty. When she answered the door, he was standing there with a dozen red roses in his hands. She threw her arms around his neck and hugged him. She wanted to kiss him, and it took all her self-control to keep from planting a big one on him. When she removed her arms from around his neck, their eyes met, and she could see the yearning in his eyes. Instead of acting on his feelings, he backed away from her.

His fear of someone getting close to him was winning out over his craving to be near her. If she only knew his true feelings for her, things between them might move at a faster pace. Instead, they were inching along, and Tempy was not sure how much longer she could deal with that.

James and Tempy needed to tell each other their true feelings; they both wanted the same thing. He wanted to tell Tempy his feelings for her; while he was in Columbia, he realized if he did not tell her his true feelings, he might lose her.

Tempy led James into the dining room, and they sat at the table as the chef brought in their dinner. James wanted her more than he could ever let her know, and his desire was getting the best of him. He knew if he ever kissed her, it would be all over; he would never let her go. He was frightened by his own feelings; he knew by the look on her face she didn't understand why he had pulled away from her in the doorway.

Tempy told James about the events of the last couple of days. She explained that she and Rick toured the properties, and he was drawing up plans for her project. She also told him about work and how she was enjoying her new freedom. She then filled him in about getting the divorce papers from Tom. James could tell she was delighted, and he was happy for her. Things in her life were straightening themselves out.

His only problem was an overwhelming yearning to kiss her, tell her his secret, and hope she could deal with it. But he was too scared she would be so mad she wouldn't forgive him for what he had done. Because of that paralyzing fear, he could not say anything, so he sat there and listened as she told him about her week. He knew in his heart if he ever gave in to his desire to kiss her, she would realize who he was.

As they ate dinner, they were happy to have an evening to themselves. Tempy did not understand why he pulled away from her after they hugged at the door. She could tell he wanted to be more than just friends, but something was holding him back, and she wondered what she had done. She knew, however, that he had spent the last eight years as a hermit, and the feelings he was experiencing now were painful for him to deal with.

Around eleven thirty, he got up to leave; he was going home to spend another night alone. He kissed her cheek and walked to his car. Tempy did not want him to go, but she knew she had to.

As James drove home, he thought about the kiss he gave Tempy at the door. He could tell she wanted to take their relationship to the next level, and despite his fear of getting close to anyone, he wanted to get closer to her too. James just did not know how to tell her his secret. They were too busy dancing around each other, not knowing how to deal with the feelings they had for each other.

James did not come in to work at all on Thursday. She thought he was avoiding her because she hugged him. She thought she had made the situation more difficult for him. She wondered if she had done something wrong at dinner and assumed he wanted to stay away from her to figure things out for himself.

Tempy talked to Shawn about clearing the land on Saturday. She asked him if he and James could come to the property on Saturday to help her clean it up. He told her they both would be there.

Chapter 16

No one had seen or heard from James since he left Tempy's house Wednesday night. He did not call Tempy or answer the phone when she tried to call him. Nobody had any idea what was going on with him. Tempy was getting worried about him. She knew he was a man of habit and stuck to his routine at all times.

When James returned home Wednesday night, Evelyn Bohannon was waiting for him inside the house. She had broken in earlier and entered his house through the garage and was waiting for him inside the kitchen door when he walked in.

As soon as he walked through the back door, she struck him across the face with the stock of the handgun she was holding.

"James, will you do me the honor of taking me to bed and making love to me?"

He looked at her and shook his head. She hit him again, harder this time.

He sat on his kitchen floor for a few minutes, trying to gather his wits.

"Evelyn, I only have eyes for one woman," he said. "I told you repeatedly for the last eight years about this. I made no secret that I wanted nobody else."

"How can that be true, when you're all over Tempy? Why can't I be one of your women? I'd do anything you ask."

"I have no interest in being involved with you, Evelyn. I am sorry. If this were thirtyfive years ago, I'd have no problem doing what you ask, but not today."

As Wednesday night turned into Thursday morning, Evelyn tried every trick she knew to get James to make love to her. She tortured him and tormented him in the hopes she could somehow break his will and get him to do whatever she wanted him to do. But nothing seemed to work. She tried all day Thursday and through Thursday night. James was still holding his own with her, but he began having second thoughts. She knew what she was doing and knew it would only take a little while longer. Sooner rather than later, he would do anything she asked him to.

Later that night, Evelyn changed her method of torment. She made James think she was Tempy. She figured that James had feelings for Tempy, and if she wanted him to make love to her, she had to convince him she was Tempy. She talked to James as though she were Tempy all night on Thursday and into the early morning hours of Friday. She was getting closer to making James believe Tempy had come to his house, and when she did, he would take her as his lover.

As Tempy drove into work that Friday morning, she was still upset about how things had gone Wednesday night. She didn't want him to feel as though she was pushing him to do anything.

When she went into the bank, Shawn came over and asked her, "Have you heard from James since Wednesday night?"

"No," she said. "Didn't you see him here yesterday?"

"No, he never made it into the bank. Now I am worried about him. Did he mention anything to you on Wednesday about going out of town yesterday?"

"No, I haven't heard from him since Wednesday night myself. That's not like him; he calls me at least once during the day."

"I've tried to call him many times in the last two days, and his phone goes straight to voicemail."

Tempy looked around the lobby of the bank and noticed Evelyn was not there, either.

"Brandi, do you know where Evelyn is?" Tempy asked.

"No," Brandi replied. "I haven't seen her since Wednesday afternoon when we left together. What's up?"

"Nobody has heard from James since Wednesday," she said, "and now Evelyn is missing too."

"Is it possible they are together?" Brandi asked.

"We're not sure what's going on yet," Tempy said; she left the teller counter and walked into Shawn's office.

"Shawn, was he seeing someone else?" Tempy asked, her voice cracking with stress.

"No," Shawn said. "You're the only woman in this bank he wanted to go out with."

"Shawn, Evelyn might have something to do with whatever is going on. Can you drive me out to James's just to make sure he is OK?"

"Sure. Give me a minute, and we can head out there now," he said.

They left the bank and got into Shawn's car.

"I have this pain in my stomach," Tempy said, "like something is wrong with James. I can't describe it, Shawn. I can tell he needs me."

"Tempy, open the glove box and hand me the two-way radio inside."

She reached inside the glove box and handed him the radio. As they drove toward James's home, Shawn radioed the local police department and told them what was going on. He notified them that one woman from the bank had not been into work in the last two days. Sheriff's dispatch radioed back they would set up their perimeter at the top of James's driveway and stand by for further instructions from him.

"10-4," he said, putting the radio down.

"Shawn, what the heck's going on?" Tempe asked.

"Eight years ago," he said, "I resigned from the US Marshals Service and joined the FBI, and they assigned me to go undercover to protect James Braden. Well, I failed him."

"No, you didn't fail," Tempy said. "How could you know someone who had the hots for him was capable of doing this? I didn't think she'd go this far."

"What do you mean? Did you hear something at the bank?"

"Yes, the women talk about him all the time, but I never thought she'd do this. This is nuts."

"You're right, this is nuts. What the heck is going on here?"

"Evelyn was upset that James and I were becoming friends. She wanted him for herself. I think she tried to get him to be with her instead of me."

"But that's insane."

"Can you think of another explanation? Like is James having an affair with her?"

"No, James would not be having an affair with another woman. He was too selfconscious, and beside that, he's in love with you."

"I'm not sure about that."

"Tempy, since you came to Pendleton, you two have danced around each other, trying not to get involved. All he wants is to be with you for the rest of his life. He did a lot to get you to Pendleton; do you really see him starting a liaison with another woman?"

Tempy looked shocked. She didn't know how to reply to Shawn's remarks. It made no sense to her, the way he acted towards her since the day she applied for the job at the bank. She wanted Shawn to hurry and get to James's house. She knew he needed her, and she wanted to be there for him. She wanted to help James and save him from Evelyn.

When Shawn got to James's, there were police cars in the driveway. Shawn got out of his car and talked to a man in a black SUV. They spoke for a few minutes, and then Shawn got back in the car.

He looked at Tempy and said, "Can you go up to James and try to get him to come to the door?"

"Sure, but if he won't come to the door, I have a key to his house."

"He gave you a key?"

"Yes."

"Do you think you can find out what is going on?"

"I can try."

Tempy got behind the wheel of Shawn's car. He lay down in the back seat so no one could see him as she drove up to the front of the house. She parked his car, walked up to the door, and knocked on it. As she waited, she could see James through the living room window. He was sitting on the sofa, and she could hear a woman's voice coming from inside.

She took the key he had given her before leaving for Columbia and opened the front door. As she walked into the house, she could hear voices in the living room. She recognized Evelyn's, and when she got to the living room door, she could see James's reflection in the hallway mirror; she also saw Evelyn next to the sofa. She had a small revolver in her hand and was talking to James.

"But why won't you have anything to do with me?" she asked.

"I told you when I purchased the bank, I only have eyes for one woman."

"Well, the only woman I've ever seen you with is Tempy, and she's only been here a couple months. Why couldn't you change your mind about dating women and pick me instead of her?"

Tempy decided to speak up.

"James are you here?" she called from outside the door.

"Yes, I'm in here with Evelyn," he replied. "She has a gun."

"Tempy, what are you doing here?" Evelyn snapped.

"Shawn and I came looking for James," she said. "He wasn't at the bank yesterday. We got worried and came to find out what's going on. Shawn and I thought something might be wrong, so we drove out here to check on him. Can I come in there to make sure he's all right?"

"No, he is fine."

"He doesn't look fine from where I am standing."

"Oh, all right," she said. "Come in for a minute and check on him, if that makes you feel better. You're the only one he wants, anyway. But maybe he would love me if I get rid of you. Maybe if you were out of the way, he'll decide he wants me instead."

"But he and I are just friends."

"No way, not with the way he looks at you all day."

"Evelyn, what are you saying? He has nothing to do with me during the day except work."

"Are you blind? He watches you from his office all the time. He lights up when you enter a room. Don't you see the way his mood changes when you are around?"

"No, I've never noticed any of that. But maybe he does have feelings for me."

"Do you have the same feelings for him?"

"Yes, I've been in love with James from the moment I met him."

Tempy walked over to the sofa. As she sat down, she looked at his face and felt around his nose and eyes. She couldn't feel any broken bones, but his face was bruised where Evelyn had hit him with the butt of the gun.

"Evelyn, he needs to see a doctor. His nose might be broken, and I can't tell what other damage you may have done."

"He's not going anywhere. He's staying here with me."

Tempy held his face in her hands and said, "James, are you all right?"

"You're not Tempy," he replied. "You're just her, trying to get me to sleep with her."

"No, baby, I am real; it is me," she whispered to him.

"Tell me something only Tempy would know and no one else."

"Before you left for Columbia, I told you I thought you were my old friend Taylor Michaels."

"Tempy, is it really you?"

"Yes, it is. Now hang on for me, OK? Sit here, out of the way."

"I'll try. Tempy, I almost did what she wanted me to do. She almost convinced me she was you."

She leaned over and whispered, "I'll be back in a minute, OK?"

She got up off the sofa and walked towards Evelyn, who was standing by the kitchen door. Just then, Tempy noticed Shawn walk into the kitchen (he had come in through the basement). She began talking to Evelyn, to keep her attention, and then Shawn came through the door and grabbed the gun out of Evelyn's hand.

"Come on, Evelyn," he said. "We need to step outside."

"What? How did you do that?" Evelyn cried.

"It doesn't matter; there are some people outside that will help you."

"Shawn, what will happen now?"

"Well, kidnapping is a serious crime; you could spend many years in jail. It also looks like you assaulted him. You're going to be held responsible."

"But he needs me to take care of him."

"He told you he only wanted one woman."

"But the only woman I've seen him with is Tempy. Is she the one he's in love with?"

"Yes, she is."

"But how? He only met her two months ago."

"Not exactly," Shawn said. "Now let's go outside."

She looked puzzled as he led her out the front door.

James held Tempy's hand and said, "What you just did was the bravest thing I've ever seen."

"Shawn asked me to do it," she said. "He needed someone to find out what was going on with you."

"How did you know?"

"I've been overhearing things at work the last couple of months."

James wanted to kiss her, but his face hurt too much. They sat in silence until Shawn returned.

"Tempy, can I talk to James for a few minutes?" he asked.

"Sure," she said. "I'll wait in the kitchen. Do either of you want something?"

"A glass of water," James said, "if you don't mind getting it for me."

"Make that two," Shawn said.

"You got it," she said. "He needs ice for his face, anyway."

"The paramedics are coming down to make sure he's OK."

"Good."

She walked into the kitchen and got two bottles of water from the refrigerator. She could see blood on the floor and in the hall, which upset her a lot. She could not help feeling all of this was because of her. Another woman had wanted James and had made no secret of her desires for the last seven weeks. Tempy felt she had missed all the signs this could happen. She was overjoyed to know James was safe. She walked back into the living room and handed each of them their water.

James grabbed her arm and said, "Thank you."

"Any time, James."

"You want to say more, don't you?" he asked.

"Yes, but after the last couple of days you've had, I can wait."

"Tempy, I can't wait to hear what you want to tell me."

She walked towards the door and said, "Shawn, I'll wait for you in the car."

"OK," Shawn said. "I'll be there in a few minutes." After she closed the door, he asked, "Jim, what happened?"

"On Wednesday night, Evelyn was waiting inside the house when I returned from dinner with Tempy."

"It looks like she hurt you."

"It's just my face. She made me believe she was Tempy. She wanted me to make love to her, but when I turned her down, she hit me in the face with the butt of the gun."

"You look like your nose is broken; did you make love to her?"

"No, but I was tempted me because I thought she was Tempy. I don't know how much longer I can keep my hands to myself. I really want her."

"Control yourself for a little while longer, my friend."

"Shawn, was that Tempy who was in here just now?"

"Yes, Jim, and she's in love with you. She put her life on the line to make sure you were OK. I think she can handle your secrets."

"My face and nose hurt."

"Any dizziness or anything of that nature?"

"No, it just hurts. I need to tell Tempy the truth."

"Yes, you do, my friend, but I think she already suspects the truth about you."

"I was thinking about telling her tomorrow night when we got back from working on the property in Oconee County."

"Maybe Evelyn's crazy stunt did some good, after all," Shawn replied.

"I don't think anything she did was good," James said with disgust in his voice.

"Well, if she got you to where you can tell Tempy the truth, that's a good thing."

"You're right, Shawn. I didn't think of that."

Just then, the paramedics came into the house to check on James.

"I'll see you later," Shawn said. "I'll be back later tonight."

"Good," James said. "I don't want to be alone in this house."

When Shawn rejoined Tempy at his car, he noticed she was crying.

"When we get off this afternoon," he said, "I'm coming back out here to spend the night with him. He'll be OK."

"Do you think it would be OK if I came by this afternoon and spent some time with him before you get here?" she asked.

"I think it would be great. He'll be ecstatic to see you again."

"Thank you. Do you think he can still help me tomorrow?"

"Yes, he's really looking forward to it."

"OK, great."

"I don't think I could keep him away tomorrow if I tried. Tempy, did you mean what you told Evelyn? Are you in love with him?"

"Yes, Shawn, I am. Don't tell him, but I know who he is. I have known for a while now."

"What do you mean?"

"He is Taylor Michaels; his family says he passed away in 2009, but it's him."

"How did you figure it out?"

"There are some things you cannot change with plastic surgery. He still walks like he did many years ago, and he still has the same attitude. When I talked to him on the phone, I could hear Taylor's voice. I won't tell him he's ready to tell me himself; I don't mind keeping his secrets."

"You're right, Tempy; you're still keeping his secrets. You're right about something else: He needs to tell you himself before you say anything to him."

"OK, I'll wait until he tells me himself."

Shawn drove Tempy back to the bank, and they finished working. For them both, the day could not end soon enough. She overheard Shawn tell the tellers what happened with James and Evelyn; he left out some details so the prosecutor could use them as evidence against Evelyn if she ever went to trial.

Tempy left the bank about five-fifteen and arrived at James's house a little after six. She walked into the house and called out his name. He did not answer her right away, and she worried that something else had happened to him. When James came out of the basement and saw her standing in the hallway, he was confused for a second and wondered where he was. He thought Evelyn had come back to torture him again. Tempy saw the look of fear in his eyes and told him who she was and said she'd stay with him until Shawn arrived.

When James realized she really was Tempy, he took her in his arms and held her for a long time. He took her to the basement, where he had his man cave. After they sat down on the sofa, she leaned over and kissed him.

He jumped up.

"Did I hurt you?" she asked.

"No, I'm OK," he said. "I'm just a little nervous."

"I'll be here for as long as you need me."

"I appreciate you coming over here. I didn't want to stay in this house alone, but if you have something else to do, I'll be OK until Shawn arrives."

Tempy figured he was trying to get her to leave because of what had happened to him. But she wanted to help him cope with the horrible events of the last three days.

"James did Evelyn use me to get you to make love to her?" she asked.

"Yes, she did."

"Do you want to tell me what she did to you?"

"She tortured me and pretended to be you to get me to make love to her. I almost did what she wanted me to do. I was losing my battle with reality and imagined she was you. She almost had me believing what she was saying. It was a good thing you walked through the door when you did this morning."

"James, I would do anything for you. I think I could have stopped this if I had told you and Shawn what I overheard her and Brandi saying in the ladies' room. She told her what she wanted to do to you, but she didn't say anything about how she planned to do it. I wouldn't blame you if you never wanted to see me again."

"Tempy, she was obsessed with me and would have found another way to try and get me to make love to her. Don't blame yourself for this.

As far as wanting to see you again, she didn't change my feelings for you at all."

As James finished his story, Tempy leaned over and kissed him softly on the forehead. Before she realized what she was doing, she began kissing him with a lot more fiery passion. James put his arm around her and kissed her back. They sat there and kissed for several minutes, and then Tempy leaned back and stared at him. All he could do was smile at her.

While they sat there, Shawn walked in. Tempy gave James one more kiss and got up to leave. Neither of them spoke about the kiss and the look Tempy had on her face afterward. If she had not known for sure before, she did now. She recognized Taylor from their kiss. After a few minutes, she told Shawn and James, she would see them the next day.

Chapter 17

Tempy asked many of her colleagues to come out to her estate on Saturday. They all agreed to help her clear debris from the land, so Rick could get started building her dream house.

Tempy drove out to the estate that Saturday morning alone. As she drove, she thought about James and their kiss the night before. When she got to the property, James and Shawn had not arrived yet. Gradually, people from the office made it to the property.

They started clearing the area, and then James and Shawn showed up. Tempy had no idea what kept them, but she was glad they finally made it. She could still see the bruises on James's face. She wondered if they hurt as much as they looked like they did.

James came over to her and said, "Good morning, Tempy. What do you need me to do?"

"Are you sure you feel up to this?" she asked.

"Yes, Tempy, I do. I want to be here. But I want to know something."

"What?"

"Did you call me 'baby' yesterday?"

"Yes, I did. Was that overstepping?"

"No, you did not overstep. I just wanted to be sure that was you and not one of Evelyn's mind games."

"James, she used me to try and get what she wanted from you. Do you remember what happened between us last night?"

"There's no way I could forget what happened between us last night. We need to talk."

"Are you sure you want to help me today?"

"Yes, but we need to talk later."

"OK, I agree. I've waited this long; I can wait a few more hours. Are you sure you want to help me clear this property?"

"Yes. It will be a perfect way to keep my mind on something besides what happened. I want to help you clear this property and get it ready to build on."

"Well, can you clear the debris from around the old house for me?"

"Sure," he said. He caught Tempy by the arm and added, "This may be the longest and hardest day I've ever had to get through."

"I can stay away from you, if that makes it easier."

"That's the last thing I need. That's not what I want at all."

After Tempy showed James what she needed him to do, Shawn came over to find out what his assignment was.

"Could you clear as much of the briars and kudzu from the entrance to the house as you can?" she asked. "The bulldozer will get a lot of this area, but they need to get onto the property first."

She was aware she had given him the hardest job there was out there. Before he got started, she told him she wanted to talk.

"Shawn is he OK?" she asked.

"When I left to go home yesterday, the paramedics told me he's fine. Just going to have a lot of bruising on his face for a while. They said he may have some emotional issues as well to work through. But other than that, he's OK. Tempy, you were amazing yesterday."

"Thank you. I was glad to help."

"He wanted to talk to you last night, but with his face like it is, I wouldn't let him out of the house. But you should talk to him."

"OK, I will."

"Did something happen before I got there last night?"

"Yes; we kissed, and it was a wonderful thing."

"Was he able to deal with it?"

"As far as I could tell. Did you mean what you told me as we were driving out to his house yesterday? He's in love with me?"

"Yes. You heard that?"

"I recall everything you told me yesterday. Are you really with the FBI?"

"Yes, but nobody else knows about that but you. There are some things about James leaving Jacksonville that nobody knows, not even him."

"Was he a witness to some crime?"

"Yes. He saw things that put his life in jeopardy. James never realized he saw anything out of the ordinary until he asked me to help him with his problems with his wife."

Tempy said, "I'll keep your secret."

"Thank you, Tempy. That's a lot to ask of you, but I know you can deal with it."

Tempy had brought a small grill and all the fixings for hamburgers to feed everyone lunch. She got the grill ready about eleven, so the hamburgers had time to cook before lunchtime. While Tempy was cooking, she thanked everybody for their help that day and then saw James standing off to the side of the house, staring at her. He was clearing the debris from around the house, but he would stop now and then to watch her. As their eyes met, she recognized the way he was looking at her; she knew the yearning in his eyes. She had seen that expression on his face many times before. Taylor would give Tempy that same tilt of his head when he wanted her to meet him in the woods behind his house. She was well aware of what he wanted, without him speaking a word. They could communicate without either of them ever saying anything. That way, there was no risk of anyone overhearing what they said.

Tempy walked over to James; when she came close to him, she said, "Are you sure you're not Taylor Michaels?"

"Well,, what makes you think I am him?"

"I don't know how; there's just something familiar about you. The way you walk, the way you are holding your head right now, and the way you kissed me last night. You look at me the same way Taylor would stare at me so many years ago. Like you, he'd never say a word, but that expression spread across his entire face; I could tell what he was thinking. I saw you get that same look on your face twice today. You have something on your mind you want to talk to me about."

"Yes, I do. Two weeks ago, when you and I were out here, how did you recognize me so fast? I was right to think, if I ever allowed you to kiss me, you would know who I was for sure."

"It's the way your left leg limps. I saw Taylor limp on that leg so many times when I was younger, and he did it for so long, it became part of the way he walked. James, you walk the same way when you're not concentrating on what's going on. When you get comfortable around people, you walk, talk, and act like Taylor. Then there is that look you have on your face right now. I noticed you look at me several times today. I cannot explain it, but your mannerisms are so familiar, and after a while, it hit me where I knew you from."

"Tempy, I cannot do this anymore. I cannot keep lying to you, even if it's by omission. You are ready to learn the truth; at least, that's the way it sounds. After what you did for me yesterday, you deserve to be told the truth. I know I'm tired of us going on like this; I am tired of disguising myself, so you don't recognize me. Then there is the matter of my trying to keep this secret from you."

"What are you talking about, James?"

"I am Taylor."

"I knew it when we were out here that first time. You convinced me last night when I kissed you, and you returned my kiss. I have to be honest about something, though; I recognized you that first day when we came out here together. Since you didn't want to admit who you are, I didn't push it. I knew when you were ready, you'd tell me the truth. I also recognized your voice after talking on the phone all those nights while you were in Columbia."

"Are you mad at me for not telling you? When you kissed me last night, I had wanted that for so long, I could not help myself. I had to give in and kiss you back."

"No, I'm not mad at you. Why didn't you tell me the truth while we out here that first afternoon? There was nobody listening to us."

"I wasn't ready to tell my version of what happened, and I didn't know if you could deal with it without getting mad at me. You might have felt like murdering me. Tempy, I am well aware what I put you and everybody else through back in Jacksonville."

"I wouldn't murder you. Might kiss you again, but there will be no bloodshed here today. James, I have loved you since I can remember. How could you even think I'd get mad at you for protecting yourself and doing what you had to do to keep your peace of mind? Hold on a minute, I'll be back."

Tempy walked over to Shawn and asked him to take over cooking the hamburgers. She said she and James had to talk about some things. Shawn agreed to take over as chef and wondered what their conversation would be about.

When she came back to James, he said, "Tempy, you are right; my left leg is killing me today. Can we sit down to talk about this?"

"Sure, let's sit on the steps of the old house for a while and talk about what happened. How bad is your face? It looks like it hurts a lot. My heart hurts to think you went through that because of me."

"My face hurts a little. What happened with Evelyn was not because of you. I don't want you to think anything that happened was your fault."

"Yes, it was. I overheard her talking to Brandi, and she sounded as though she was planning something. I should have mentioned something to you or Shawn about what I heard."

"It's OK, Tempy. I will be fine."

"Are you sure?"

"I am."

"I don't think I could handle it if you were not OK."

"Do you love me that much that you hurt when I hurt?"

"I do."

She felt so responsible about what happened the day before to James. She felt guilty about what happened to him. She grabbed him and kissed him to make sure he was OK.

Tempy had known in her heart she was right, and she wanted to see her old friend again so much, it hurt. She tingled with anticipation of learning the truth about what happened to him all those years ago.

Their eyes met; she put her hand on his and turned to him, so they were face to face.

"Taylor Anthony Michaels Jr., I have loved you since we were kids. You changed your name, changed your face, changed your hair, and they even changed your eye color. But do you know what? Even with all the changes they made, they overlooked one crucial thing: They didn't change the way you walk and look at me. Nobody could ever change the way we felt about one another. For weeks, we both suffered because we knew in our souls we wanted to be together."

"Is that how you figured it out?"

"In a way, it is."

"Could anybody else figure it out the way you did?"

"Yes, I can think of a few people who could figure out your secret if they were around, you long enough, just like I did."

"Would you mind if we don't invite our old friends to our home?"

"James, I will be fine if we keep us between us."

"OK, but that's not fair to you."

"We'll figure it out. Before you start your story, can I ask you something?"

"Sure."

"Why do you stay so close to Shawn?"

"He is my bodyguard. He knows everything there is to know about me."

James got up off the steps and walked around to stretch his leg, which was bothering him. Tempy was thinking the old house was an ironic place to find out what happened to James way back when in Jacksonville. It reminded her of the hideout in the woods he built all those years ago. This house reminded her of sneaking around in the woods when they were teenagers.

James could not believe he was about to have this conversation. It was the hardest conversation he thought he'd ever have. James and Shawn had spoken that morning about the secrets James had been keeping from Tempy. While they were driving out there that morning, they decided she was ready for him to tell her.

He looked at her for a few minutes, which seemed to be the longest few minutes of Tempy's life; she thought he was going to change his mind about telling her the truth. But then he began to tell what happened back in Jacksonville.

James started his narrative with an apology. He had seen her reaction when Beth insulted her and told her Tom wanted a divorce. He never wanted to be the source of pain like that ever again. He kept thinking back to when they were teenagers and his part in ever making her feel the way she felt about herself.

"Tempy, I am so sorry for how I treated you when we were kids. I'm also sorry that Evan raped you all those years ago, and I didn't do anything about it. But most of all, I am sorry for never telling you the truth about my feelings for you. I did what my mother asked me to do. I have wished so many times I had told her I wanted to live my life, just like she wanted to live hers. I love you, Julia Temperance Brewer. Always have, always will."

Tempy placed her index finger over his lips, and he kissed it.

She looked at him, mesmerized by his big green eyes, and said, "Well, then, if we are telling each other the truth, I knew what our parents were making us tell each other. My parents were as much to blame as yours were. They were involved as much as yours. I loved you. I know, I told you on more than one occasion. I couldn't hide my feelings for you as easy as you could. Taylor, I could have told you I was having the same issues you were. You were not alone. We should have talked about how we felt and not given in to what others wanted us to feel, even if they were our parents. We did each other a huge disservice back then."

Tempy paused and then found the words to capture her feelings about him.

"We cannot just pick up today where we left off back then. We did those things because our parents forced us to. We need to see if the feelings we shared then are still true or just something else they twisted. First, though, I want to know how you wound up here."

"All of it?"

"I want to know every gory detail of what brought us to this point."

"OK, do you think you can handle it?"

"After yesterday, I think I can handle almost anything life has to throw at me."

"I'll begin at the beginning. After Scarlett and I got divorced, I wanted to find you, although I didn't think you wanted to hear from me ever again. You made it clear when I was married that you wanted more from me, and I didn't know how to tell you I wanted the same thing. I couldn't tell you about my feelings for you, and I thought that would spare you any more pain.

"So after my divorce, I met Betsey Moore and fell in love with her. It was not like how I felt for you or Scarlett—but I could live with the choice I had to make. For a while, she made me happy.

"After my mother died, I wrecked my car, not once, not twice, but three times. The third time, I was in the hospital with a broken leg, and my doctors gave me hydrocodone for the pain while I was there. When I was discharged, they gave me a prescription for a threemonth supply. When it rained, the pain in my leg was unbearable. I would take one for the pain when I needed it. I had no way of knowing Betsey was putting them into my food. After two months, my leg was almost healed, the pain was subsiding, and I felt I was well enough to go to town alone.

"One Saturday, I decided to drive into town. I got into my car and started down the driveway. When I got to the end of the driveway, I discovered I had no brakes. My car went across the road and landed in a ditch. I blacked out and came to in the hospital. The Emergency Room nurses told me my codeine levels were through the roof; I had three broken ribs, another broken leg, and a punctured lung.

"I was admitted to the hospital, and my doctor came to see me; he asked me if I was trying to kill myself. I told him I didn't believe in suicide; it's the coward's way out. He suggested we call the Marshals Service, and I agreed to speak with them. At that point, I didn't know what to think.

"After the doctor left my room, I fell asleep. When I woke up, Betsey was sitting beside me. The nurse came in a few minutes later to check my vitals. Apparently, she saw something in my vital signs she did not like. She asked Betsey if she would wait outside while she finished checking my vitals and helping me to the restroom. When she asked me if I wanted Betsey to return, I told her I did. What else was I going to do? If I had said no, she would know I knew what she did.

"The next morning during breakfast, three tall, muscular gentlemen wearing black suits walked into my hospital room. They were US Marshals: Shawn Mitchell, whom you know, Bruce Henry, and Christopher Parker. Shawn was the agent in charge of my case. He asked if they could have a seat so the four of us could talk for a while.

"Shawn told me they had investigated my case and found someone had tampered with my car; the brake lines were cut. And then she told me my doctor said my codeine levels were through the roof, even though I only took the prescribed amount.

"Sean then said they checked my home and found several bags of hydrocodone pills in Betsey's medicine cabinet. There was also high levels of codeine in the leftovers from the refrigerator. They suspected she was trying to kill me, or she liked the feeling she got when she took care of me; they call that the Florence Nightingale syndrome. That's when he told me they wanted to put me in the witness protection program."

"Why?" Tempy asked.

"Because the Marshals Service thought Betsey might be trying to murder me or one of her kids. But first, I had to recuperate from the accident. They told me they'd be in touch after I regained my strength.

"It took almost seven months for me to fully recover from that accident. But after I did, Shawn sent me a text message with detailed instructions on what they wanted me to do. He began by having me convince everyone that Betsey had me hooked on the prescription drugs. Everyone had to believe the agony I was experiencing from my last accident was just too much for me to handle. I followed his directions, and everyone believed I had given up and was only interested in the pills."

"One afternoon, Daddy came by the house to check on me. I could see he was furious with me for the way I had let my part of the business slide. He was also disappointed for what I was letting happen to myself.

He asked me what was going on, and I told him. I explained that I had to ask him to go along with something, but I needed him to promise me something first."

"He said, 'Anything, son, you know that."

"I told him we needed to go somewhere and talk, and he said OK.

"I told Betsey that Daddy and I were going to the store and would be back in a little while. She said OK.

"As we left the driveway and rode towards town, I laid the entire plan out for him. He looked as though he would faint. I told him I needed him to make sure Tempy heard of my death from someone in the family. I didn't want her finding out by accident.

"I also told him that I loved her and wanted him to convince the coroner and sheriff's department that I killed myself.

"We drove back to the house, and he played his part perfectly.

"A couple months later, Shawn let me know he had everything in place. As far as Betsey knew, I was as high as a kite from all the pills she had been giving me. One day, I drove to the store, but this time, I was not alone. Shawn was in the back seat of my car. He had given me padding for my knees so I wouldn't get hurt as badly as I had the last time. I started down the driveway and again found I had no brakes. I hit the ditch across the road doing about forty miles an hour. I hit my head on the steering wheel and was knocked out, and Shawn pulled me out of the car.

"After a few minutes, a black car pulled up; some men got out and put me inside. They put another body in the front seat of my car, and when the paramedics arrived, they pronounced me dead. They took the body out of the car before Betsey came down to see if I was all right.

"Shawn delivered the news of my death to my father. Because they sent the body to the crime lab, they just had a memorial service for me.

"Daddy knows I am alive, but he doesn't know where I am. Shawn calls him every couple of months and lets him know I'm OK. I would love to be able to visit him sometime, but that's not possible. Someone else might see me, and then my secret would be out."

"Taylor, if I weren't so happy to see you, I would wring your neck myself."

"What do you want to do, now that you know my secret?"

"I'd like to throw you down on the ground and have my way with you. We have a chance here to start over. Let's take it. That is, if you want to."

"If I want to? Are you joking? I was afraid you couldn't handle the truth about me. Are you serious?"

"I am serious, but I have a request."

"What's that?"

"I can't stand the name James. If it's all right with you, I'd like to call you something else; how about Alex? It is your middle name, and I would like something that is unique to us."

"That's fine with me, as long as no one else calls me that."

James, soon to be called Alex, just sat, and stared at Tempy for a long time. He loved the way she made him feel about himself and the world around him. He realized that he still loved her.

Chapter 18

James continued, "After Shawn and I faked my death, he resigned from the Marshals Service and joined the FBI, and then he helped me get to where I am today. He was assigned to protect me from the three men he saw shoot a young boy. One of these men had approached his wife to help with killing me."

He pulled a two-way radio out of his pocket and called Shawn, who was finishing up with the hamburgers.

"Shawn," he said, "Tempy and I are walking up to the other property for a little while. We want to look at the plantation house before we finish here."

Tempy heard, but her mind was elsewhere, and she was not paying attention to Shawn as he responded, "OK. Do you two want a ride up there?"

"No, we just want to walk and be by ourselves. She knows the entire story; I told her just a few minutes ago."

"Did you tell her, or did she find out for herself? How did she take it?"

"She figured it out and took it better than I hoped she would. Last night, we kissed, and I could tell at that moment she knew who I was; she didn't say anything, but I could tell by the way she looked at me she had figured it out.

"I wasn't ready to tell her, but now that I did, I'm glad it's out of the way. I felt guilty about keeping her in the dark. My conscience got the better of me, and I couldn't lie to her anymore."

"Does she think she can handle your secret?"

"Yes, she does. She wants to take it slow for now."

"Well,, at least she wants to try."

"Yes, it's a start. If we're not back before you finish there, meet us at the other house."

"You got it, my friend."

Shawn put away the radio and returned to the grill. Barry came over to say hello.

"How's it going?" he asked Shawn.

"It's going good," he replied. "We're getting Tempy's property ready for Rick Webber to begin construction. Want to help me finish up these burgers?"

"Sure, be glad to. Where is James?"

"He and Tempy are at the other house."

"Did he tell her the truth about him yet?"

"No, she already knows."

"How did she find out?"

"Jim said she noticed some familiar things about him and figured it out several weeks ago."

When the hamburgers were ready, Shawn called everyone in the eat. They ate and talked amongst themselves; someone asked Shawn about the bruises on James's face, and he told them what happened the day before, explaining that Evelyn did that to him. No one there could believe it, except Brandi. She told Shawn about their conversations over the last couple of months and said she had been expecting something, but not that.

"James was always upfront with his feelings about getting involved with women," she said. "I had feelings for him too, but he made it clear that he only had eyes for one other woman, so I found someone else."

While everyone finished eating lunch, Shawn checked the property and saw they did everything Rick had put on his list. He told the bank employees they could return to Pendleton.

After everyone left, Shawn drove up to the Calhoun property. They got out their car and waited for Tempy and James to come out of the woods. After a short wait, they did. James had disregarded the pain in his face and kissed Tempy. They found it hard to control themselves after that kiss, but they managed somehow.

Tempy was surprised to see Shawn had finished working on the other property.

She looked at Shawn and said, "I first thought there was something going on with you two. I couldn't put my finger on what I found so familiar about him, but when I saw him limping, I knew who he was. You changed a lot of things about him, but you forgot to teach him how to walk again. He still walks just like he did all those years ago back home when we were teenagers."

"You know that help-wanted poster you found from the bank? It didn't show up by accident. We had been following you for some time, making things in your life work out so you had to leave and come to Pendleton. We left the South Carolina brochure at the convenience store where you got gas. We couldn't leave it to chance that you learned about the job at the bank."

"Shawn, I should be mad about being manipulated like that. But I'm not, since I want to spend every waking minute I can with this man."

"Keep spending time together and become friends again," Shawn suggested. "After you become friends, let things follow their natural course."

They all walked on into the Calhoun mansion.

Chapter 19

Tempy was dealing with a lot of emotions hitting her all at once. She was so grateful she had found her old friend again, and he told her the truth. She couldn't let go of Alex's hand. She was sad because he could never go home and visit his father. She vowed to find a way for them to spend time with each other again.

Tempy's other property included an eighteenth-century antebellum home. She took the key and unlocked the front door. When she went inside, she was awestruck; the place left a lump in her throat every time she looked at its sheer grandeur. Even though she had been through the house many times before, it still took her breath away. She was so glad the plantation evaded the wrath of Sherman during the concluding months of the Civil War. She read the stories of his march through Georgia; he didn't leave a lot behind when he marched his men to Savannah, but this house remained as it had been the day John Calhoun took his wife and kids to Alabama.

The staircase started as a regular set of steps on the ground floor and then opened at the top to lead to rooms on both sides.

Tempy said, "I treasure this old house and already know how I want to remodel it. I also know what I want to do with the property."

Alex and Shawn looked at each other and asked her the same question at the same time: "What, Tempy?"

"I want to return it to its original grandeur. I want to make this house and estate into a resort. I want something my family can be proud of for generations to come."

Alex asks her a simple question: "Why don't you do it?"

"I am," she said, "but I have a problem. I can't admit to owning anything during the next forty days; if I put these properties in my name before my divorce's waiting period is over, Tom can tell the judge I inherited them while we were still husband and wife. I don't owe Tom Pierce half of anything else that belonged to my family. He has taken enough from me as it is."

James still hadn't told Tempy he had bought the property in Jacksonville; he was waiting to give her that news later.

"But Tempy, you were given the estate after you and Tom separated."

"Yes, I know that, but I want no problems with Tom. If he finds out about my life here, he will come after what I inherited. It's in my best interest to keep the property as it is for now."

"Well, we could put the business into the bank's name while we wait till the divorce is final."

"Alex, I'm sorry, but I cannot get past what Tom put me through for the last few years. I can't run the risk of another man taking everything I have from me again. I don't think I will be able to trust like that again, not even you. Not now, anyway. It's too soon after Tom took everything from me; the pain is still too raw."

Alex said, "We will figure it out, Tempy. But in the meantime, I could be your business partner."

"Now there's something I have no problem with. I want to spend as much time with you as I can. I want to be sure we can be friends again; were we really attracted to each other, or did someone else force us into it? I was hoping you'd agree to be my business partner. I'll have Barry draw up the paperwork to that effect when I put the homes in my name."

She gave him a hug and then turned to Shawn.

"Shawn, could you give me a ride back to the other property? I want to make sure we finish there so it's ready for Rick to start."

"I can give you a ride, Tempy, but we finished the list Rick gave you before lunch. Everyone already took off and headed home for the day."

"Thank you, I'm a little tired myself. It's been a long time since I hiked that much."

Shawn drove them back to the property, and after dropping her off, he and Alex headed back to Pendleton.

Tempy was glad the property was so far out of town that day. During the long drive back, she thought about what had taken place with Tom, with Evelyn, with Betsey, and even with Evan when she was a teenager. She also thought about what she was feeling for Alex. She wanted to give their new relationship a chance, and she was curious to see how he fit into her plans. She had no intention of forcing herself on him; she wanted Alex to figure out for himself what he needed and wanted from their relationship.

She had not realized that he was the driving force behind bringing her to Pendleton. He had known months earlier that he wanted her, and he was just waiting for her to catch up with him so he could take care of her for the rest of her life.

Tempy had a lot of ideas running through her head about what she would do with the smaller house. She wanted Alex to be a part of those plans. It all depended on where he wanted their relationship to go. She realized they had a lot to take care of before they could get back to where they were years ago. It had been a long time, but Alex already knew what he wanted to see happen between himself and Julia Temperance Brewer.

When she got back to the condo, Alex was waiting outside her door. She invited him in so they could talk in private.

He followed her inside, and after she shut the door, she turned to him and said, "Alex let's start over, the two of us. Take it one day at a time, and see where we wind up."

"OK," he said. "I'll respect your wishes for now."

"You are aware of the grounds Tom used for his divorce; it really hurt me."

"Yes, I am. Do you better about yourself now?"

"Yeah, a little. It still hurts when I think that people might see me as the whore, he portrayed in those divorce papers."

"All that matters is that I know the truth. I can see the real you, even if they don't. Most of what he did, he did to hurt you and make you doubt yourself. Don't worry about it; it's the past, and we are together now."

They sat on her comfortable couch and talked about what they wanted now that she knew the truth about him. Alex didn't mind giving her the time she needed to work out what was going on in her life. He already knew where he wanted things to go between them.

After a while, Tempy felt hungry and asked Alex, "Do you want something to eat before you go home and spend the rest of the night alone? Would you like to spend a little more time alone with me?"

"Yes, I could go for a sandwich. It's been a long time since lunch. And I'd like to stay a while longer. I am not ready to go home to that big empty house. After last week, I don't think I want to ever go back there at all."

"We can start with the rest of tonight, getting acquainted with each other slowly."

"Slow sounds wonderful. I don't want to press things with you and scare you away."

Tempy and Alex sat and chatted about everything that night. Alex explained why he was so close to Shawn. The Marshals Service trained him to be the branch manager so he could be close to James.

"It turned out to be a good arrangement," he said, "but I want something more out of life than my only friend being my bodyguard."

Tempy thought, *I'll be your bodyguard, if that's your problem.*

She was glad Alex didn't hear her and smiled, thinking he'd be terrified if he heard her proposal.

During that night, they caught up on a lot of the experiences of the last thirty-two years. They seemed to make a new beginning. They could become friends who want to spend time with one another, friends who wanted to know each other well before they tried being anything else. Tempy sincerely hoped they would find love with each other, but there was a long way to go before she could trust her heart. First, she had to get past the memories she still wrestled with of their relationship years before. She wanted to be sure she and Alex were friends, not just picking up where they left off.

She hoped he couldn't see she was still wildly attracted to him. She almost wanted to throw caution to the wind, throw him on the floor, and have her way with him, but she knew taking it slow was a much better idea. She could not stop the feelings building up inside her. She wanted him to wrap his arms around her and let her get lost in them. However, she resisted being captivated by him for the time being. After being held captive, he might not be ready to start a relationship with anybody right now.

They stopped talking about three thirty, and Alex retired to the guest room. He slept late, and when he came downstairs, Tempy was fixing lunch for them. She had watched him sleep after she woke up and felt her love resurfacing towards him; she struggled to keep it in check until she knew what he wanted. She already knew without a shadow of a doubt what she wanted for their future together. As he watched her fix lunch, she wondered what he was thinking about. He wanted to take her in his arms like he used to.

After they finished eating, they talked for a little while, and then he said he needed to go home and get some work done. He was well aware he could get nothing done as long as he was with Tempy. He did not want to leave her, but he knew deep down he had to. Before he walked out of the condo, he kissed her. When their mouths met, he knew he was where he always wanted to be. He pulled away from her and went to his car; he knew if he didn't leave right then, they would wind up in bed together, and he didn't think she was ready for them to start an intimate relationship yet.

James himself did not know how he felt about having sex with anybody so soon after Evelyn's torture. He was still having trouble figuring out what was real after Evelyn's mind games. She figured out that Tempy was the key to James's heart and used that to get James to a place where he would have given himself to her, thinking she was Tempy. James had to find help for what he was going through, or it would pull him apart.

Chapter 20

James knew deep down in his heart that Tempy was right. He knew she wanted to do things right this time. As he drove home that Sunday afternoon, he decided they would do it her way (since his way worked out so well when they were younger). It took all he could do, sitting in front of that cozy fire, not to act on his feelings for her. He didn't think she could miss the fire in his eyes, the blushing of his cheeks, or the attraction he still felt for her.

James used the rest of his Sunday afternoon to figure out what he wanted from his relationship with Tempy. He wished he had made better decisions years ago; he had no desire to make the same mistakes again. He decided what to tell the staff at the bank about him and Tempy. He was not keen on anyone knowing he cared about Tempy until she was ready to tell them herself. James meant what he had said to her; he would allow her to set the pace of their relationship, but it was so nice to enjoy the company of someone other than Shawn. James looked forward to seeing Tempy at work and at home.

When James got into work on Monday morning, Shawn was already waiting in his office, hoping to hear how the rest of James's weekend had gone. He wondered if there could be something between him and Tempy again.

"Well, how did it go after I left you Saturday afternoon? Do you think she can keep your secret?"

James laughed at Shawn. He had done very little laughing in the eight years he had been in Pendleton. It felt good to laugh. Shawn liked what he heard; he was seeing parts of his friend's personality he never saw before. He had never heard him laugh in all the time he had known him.

"Shawn, she kept my secrets for many years; at one time in our lives, she was my secret. I think she can handle this one."

"But what if she doesn't want to?"

"I'll cross that bridge when I get to it, OK?"

"OK, my friend. I am here if you need me."

"I know you are, but I think Tempy can handle my secrets. Thanks for being here for me. We have a problem, though."

"What is that, Jim?"

"I keep thinking about the suggestions Evelyn put into my head; I'm having trouble telling if it's Tempy talking or her."

"Wow, she came close to convincing you she was Tempy, huh?"

"Very; if Tempy hadn't walked in that morning, I have no idea how that situation would have turned out. Evelyn almost convinced me she was Tempy. I might have made love to her right there in my living room."

"Maybe you should call a psychologist to help you get over this."

"That's not a bad idea."

Shawn called a friend and set up a meeting for James with a psychologist. They gave him an appointment with Dr. Smith for that Monday afternoon.

James had several meetings before seeing Dr. Smith. He found it hard keeping his mind off what happened in his home last week. He needed to get Evelyn out of his head. He wanted her out of his head; he was having trouble figuring out what was real and what was made up.

He sat on the psychologist's couch and told him what happened the week before, how a woman pretended to be the woman he loved to get him to make love to her. And now he could not tell if he was living in the present or still being manipulated by this other woman's suggestions.

As James talked to Dr. Smith, he understood that his mind wanted Tempy so much that his subconscious was playing tricks on him, using Evelyn's suggestions.

Dr. Smith told James, "Your problem may never go away, or maybe Tempy will wipe the suggestion out of your mind forever with just the simple act of making love to you."

James hoped the doctor was right.

Tempy drove back to the bank. She had to stop by her other businesses to see how they were doing. Tempy made a point of visiting them every Monday afternoon before she went to lunch. She made it a point to sit and listen to their concerns about their jobs and the way business was being conducted.

Chapter 21

Tempy arrived at work about eight thirty that Tuesday morning. She slept like a baby the entire weekend after James told her the truth about himself. She was feeling loved, wanted, and at peace with herself. She was afraid that things were going too good at the bank; something might come her way and set her happiness back. She wondered why it always had to work out like that. Why couldn't she just let go for a change and not let anything bother her? She decided that morning that whatever was coming, she would handle it and keep moving forward with her life. She'd let no one, not even Tom Pierce, get in her way of finding happiness; for the first time, she would make the life she always wanted.

Before James went to the bank, he stopped by Dr. Smith's office. He was still having problems telling what was real with Tempy and what Evelyn had planted as a suggestion to get him to make love to her. He told him about his dreams and the difficulty he was having telling reality from fiction. He asked his doctor what he could do to make all the bad dreams go away.

"This is not much help," Dr. Smith said, "but if you let nature take its course between you and Tempy, you will solve your own problems."

"But how do I know for sure if it's Tempy or something Evelyn put into my head?"

"James, you will know when it happens if it is real or not."

"Most of the time, I feel like I am dreaming and cannot wake up from a nightmare."

"That will go away when you least expect it. When Tempy is ready, she'll make your life happy again."

"I hope so. I love her with all my heart. I just want to throw her on the floor and have my way with her."

"Show her how you feel."

"Things keep cropping up to keep us apart."

"Try to get close to her without scaring her to death."

"Well, I didn't bring her to Pendleton to lose her now."

"I spoke with Shawn about you and Tempy. He thinks you need to tell her what is in your head and in your heart."

"Doctor, I have loved this woman for as long as I can remember. Our parents did not want us together, so we had to see each other whenever we could in secret."

"Have you told her how you feel?"

"No, I think it will scare her to death, and she'll be out of my life forever."

"You will never know how she feels about you until you try. You cannot be a recluse and hide from her and everyone else anymore. Try to be the person you were before you left Jacksonville."

"What if I revert to my old ways?"

"Then you'll know you don't love just one person."

Tempy wondered what Beth would attempt to talk Tom into doing now that the judge signed the divorce papers. She had two messages from Beth that morning, saying she wanted to talk to her. So she picked up the phone and called Tom to find out what he wanted. She was happy with her new life, and what he wanted no longer mattered to her;

she would find happiness no matter what Tom tried to do. His sister made all his decisions, and Tempy was no longer a part of that life.

Beth answered Tom's phone and told Tempy that Tom wanted nothing to do with her. "Well, that's not true," she said. "He wants you to give him a little more money."

"How much more, Beth?"

"Another two hundred and fifty thousand dollars will be enough for him to live off of for the rest of his life."

"I don't have that kind of money. Anyway, I don't feel owe him anything else. He got one hundred and eight thousand dollars from the mortgage of my home and the money he borrowed from my father. How much more does he want? Or is it you who wants more from me?"

"We figured if you could come up with the first payment, you could come up with this."

"I am not giving him another dime."

"We are on our way to Pendleton to talk with you about it, and we should be there within the hour."

"Really? I will let you know then what my lawyer has to say about this."

Tempy hung up the phone and went downstairs for her morning meeting with James. She noticed Shawn's office was empty when she walked by and figured they were both in James's office. She walked to the door, and there was a "Do not disturb" sign on it.

Tempy turned around to go back upstairs but then changed her mind and opened the door.

"Shawn, does the 'Do not disturb' sign apply to me? I'd like talk to him for a few minutes, OK?"

"No problem," Shawn said. "You can talk to him any time you want; you always make him smile."

"Now don't go very far; I have a feeling we will need your help with other problems before this is over."

"Sure, I'll be in my office if you need me; just buzz me, and I'll come right back. Tempy, you know that 'Do not disturb' sign doesn't apply to you."

She placed her hand on Shawn's arm as he started out the door and whispered to him, "Thank you for everything you have done for him over the years."

"Not a problem," he said as he walked out the door. "I love him too, and I've never seen him as happy as he is today. I heard him laugh a little while ago, something I've never heard him do. I have a feeling the change in his mood today is all thanks to you."

Shawn shut the door behind him. He knew neither one of them wanted anyone outside their close circle of friends to know their secrets, so he would help them keep their personal lives just that: personal.

"Alex, I have a problem with Tom."

"What happened?"

"When I got in this morning, I had several messages from him. I called him back, and guess who answered his phone again? Beth told me he wants another two hundred and fifty thousand dollars. And to top that off, they are on their way here to collect."

"Tempy, I can tell this bothers you. The waiting period in your divorce is over. I don't think he can get any more from you since the judge signed your divorce agreement."

"I don't want to scare you," she said, "but I will say this anyway: I love you. I needed to hear that. I was having the same thoughts, but I wanted someone besides myself to tell me I was on the right track with what I was thinking."

"You are."

"I need to call Barry and get him over here before Beth and Tom arrive from Manchester."

"That's a good idea; call him and tell him what's going on with these two."

He took Tempy's hand. As he calmed her down, she noticed the scars on his hands. She looked at him with questions in her eyes; she wanted to know how he got those scars. She never verbalized the questions, but he knew what she wanted to know.

"They made those when they tried to alter my fingerprints and palm prints. They tried to erase all evidence of my ever being Taylor Michaels."

"Is this why you've never gotten close to another woman?"

"Yes, somewhat. I cannot answer their questions about why I have these scars, and I cannot tell them who I used to be. I don't have to answer questions with you; you already know the answers. Heck, you've known me for as long as I can remember. There is also the fact I have never stopped loving you. After I purchased the bank, I told every woman who ever approached me that I had eyes for one woman and one woman only. Can you handle the scars on my hands and face, or do they disgust you?"

"I can handle the scars on your hands and the ones behind your ears. What I cannot handle is the way you had to lie to your family and me because of something I said to you all those years ago. You were mistaken; I wanted to see you again. I feel as responsible for what happened to you with Betsey as you do for what happened with Evan."

"Do you think you would ever tell me no again?"

"That's a loaded question because the answer to your question is no. So, let's say I would not tell you no again for the reason you are talking about. I am glad they could not erase all trace of Taylor."

"Why? Do you mean what you mean?"

"Yes, I do. You know exactly what I am telling you. We know each other very well. If they wiped out all trace of Taylor, I would never have been able to find him again. My heart feels better knowing he is alive.

Alex, I want to know just how alive he is." As she finished her statement, she winked at him.

Alex stared at her, wondering if she really meant it. He knew the door was open for a relationship between them, but he wasn't sure she meant what she just said. He hoped she did. His heart was pounding in his chest like a bass drum.

"Tempy, can you find it in your heart to keep my secrets again? Would you want to do that?"

She stared at him for what seemed like forever. Then she leaned toward him and whispered, "For the rest of my life."

With that said, they stared into each other's eyes, yearning to take the relationship to the next level. They both knew this was not the time or place to act on their feelings. But neither of them seemed to care; however, just as they were about to throw caution to the wind, there was a knock at James's door.

Startled back to reality, they forced themselves to put their feelings on hold one more time.

Shawn entered before James had a chance to ask him to come in.

"Have you two figured out our latest mess?" he asked.

"Well, we have," Tempy said. "A little. We'll try to figure out the rest of our mess later."

As she spoke, she had the biggest grin on her face she ever had. Tempy knew if Shawn had not disturbed them at that moment, things could have gotten out of hand. She had wanted him to kiss her so bad, her whole body ached, but she knew the bank wasn't the place for anything to happen. It should happen when they were alone and on their own time, not where the entire world could see what was happening between them.

Tempy picked up James's phone and called Barry to fill him in on the latest developments with Tom. He was surprised to hear she was being asked for additional support and let her know he'd be at the bank when Tom and Beth arrived.

Tempy walked over to the teller counter and told them how she wanted things handled when Beth and Tom arrived. They said they'd let her know the minute they got there. As Tempy was speaking with the tellers, James walked up behind her, startling everyone; when he came into the bank that morning, they all gasped when they saw his bruised face. He was, however, coming out of his shell.

"I'll see you in a little while," Tempy said.

"Hey, you want to have lunch with me today?"

"Sure," she said as she headed towards the stairs that led up to her office.

Tempy sat in her office and recalled what almost happened. She wanted James to kiss her, but she also feared it was too soon for them to start their relationship over again. To her, it was still too soon to separate what happened when they were younger with what was happening now. James and Shawn convinced her they still needed more time to understand their new relationship.

A little before eleven, Beth and Tom arrived. They approached the teller counter and asked to see Temperance Brewer Pierce (two weeks before, when the judge signed the divorce papers, Tempy had her name changed back to Brewer, but Tom and Beth didn't bother respecting that change. Brandi called Tempy and informed her that the two of them were waiting to see her in the lobby. She also told her that Barry was on his way to the bank.

Tempy told Brandi to show Beth and Tom to her office.

As Brandi led them up the stairs to Tempy's office, she could see that Beth's face was puckered and she was trying to impress upon everyone she was angry and ungiving.

Tempy invited Tom and Beth to have a seat and said, "Brandi, please ask Barry to join us the minute he gets here."

"I will."

"Would either of you like a drink before we get started?"

"No," Beth said in her nastiest voice.

Just then, James brought Barry into Tempy's office. Barry stopped in his office to say hello before coming upstairs to their meeting. After they sat down, Tempy spoke.

"Beth, Tom, this is Barry Wright, my attorney. He will handle the request you made earlier today."

"Good to meet you."

Barry looked at Beth and wondered why she thought she could get more money for Tom after the judge already signed the divorce agreement.

"You are aware a judge already signed the agreement, which means my client is no longer responsible to your brother for anything; she does not have to tell him anything she is doing. Let's be clear with one another: if we give you anything, it will be out of the goodness of our hearts, with no legal connotations implied by the whole agreement."

"We already spent the money she gave him with the settlement."

"What did you spend all that money on?" Barry asked.

"We bought him a house to live in; now he needs something besides his small Social Security check to take care of himself for the rest of his life."

"Why so much for a house for one person to live in?"

"He found someone who wants to take care of him, but she wants to be taken care of. Living with him and him on SSI, she does not have the choice of working herself. So they need a nest egg to fall back on."

James almost lost his balance and fell out of the big leather chair in the back of Tempy's office. Tempy could not help smiling at him. She was just as shocked as James was by Beth's brazen request.

"Why do you think my client owes you one more time to take care of your brother?"

"He took care of her for almost thirty years; now it is her turn to take care of him."

"I don't see it that way, but I know you will keep hounding her for money until she gives him more, so I might as well suggest she pay him a lump sum now this one last time."

"She looks like she can afford it with this cushy new job."

"Tempy, can you come up with the money she's asking for?"

Tempy looked at James, and he nodded his head in agreement; they would run this two hundred and fifty thousand dollars the same way they did the first payment. He got up and excused himself so he could get the paperwork started for the money. James didn't want Tom or Beth to know Tempy could come up with that money and a lot more. He was ready for this nightmare to be over for her.

Barry finished talking to Tom and Beth, but before he left her office, Tempy asked him if she could see him that afternoon. To her surprise, he said yes and called his secretary while he stood there. He spoke to her for a minute and then turned to Tempy and said he could see her at two thirty that afternoon.

Then Barry said, "I don't know what's different about James, but he seems a lot happier today than he was the last time I saw him. Where did he get those bruises on his face?"

"Not right now," Tempy said. "I will tell you about them this afternoon."

"OK, see you then."

Barry could not figure out what was going on between Tempy and James. He excused himself and left Tempy's office. A few minutes later, James came back with a cashier's check for Tom for another two hundred and fifty thousand dollars.

Beth and Tom assumed James had loaned her the money because she had nothing in her bank account when she left Manchester.

Beth turned to Tom and whispered to him, "That was too easy; we'll be back for more."

"Why?" he replied. "We got the two hundred and fifty thousand we asked for. Why not just leave her alone?"

"It's time she paid for all the suffering she put you through," Beth remarked.

"I suppose, but I don't remember being all that miserable," Tom said.

Tempy sat back in her big chair and wondered just how many more times they would expect her to come up with money for Tom. She decided to talk to Barry about how to make them stop asking her for money.

Tempy overheard Beth tell Tom that she had gotten the money from James, and they would go after him next. She was afraid there would be more to come. She was unsure when that other shoe would drop, and they would leave her trying to find another two hundred and fifty thousand dollars. She decided she had enough of the Pierces; she would take the bull by the horns and put a stop to them ever asking her for another dime. She would take care of the problem before Beth went to James for more money.

Chapter 22

Barry noticed the bruises on James's face that morning, but he didn't say anything about them. He was not about to pry into his friend's business until he was ready to tell him about what was going on. If James didn't want him to know what was going on, he'd respect those wishes. He assumed that when James was ready, he would tell him how he got the bruises. He'd also tell him what was going on with Tempy. Barry had been friends with James long enough to realize he would let him in on his secrets when he was ready to. He mentioned the bruises to Tempy on his way out of her office. She said she'd explain as best she could when she saw him that afternoon.

Something about their relationship still troubled him, though. James had only known this woman a couple months, but he saw a side of him he never had seen before. He liked the way Tempy was affecting James and hoped she and James would become better friends. He saw how good she was for him and wanted whatever effect she was having on him to continue. It was time he had happiness in his life. Barry thought for a long time that James needed to get out more. He always thought he was too much of a recluse, and if this is who he needed to bring him out of his shell, he was all for it.

Tempy walked into Barry's office and said, "Good afternoon, Barry. How are you doing today?"

"I'm fine, thanks," he answered.

"Everyone at the bank is fine," she said. "James is laughing and smiling for a change. Shawn and I are working on him to talk to the other employees; we're not there yet, but maybe soon."

"Well, if he's coming out of his shell, that's all that matters. I don't understand how you caused such a change in him so quickly, but he'll give me the whole story when he's ready. Did you want me to do something else for you?"

"Yes, but first, you asked me about the bruises on James's face. I can explain what happened. Evelyn kidnapped him last Wednesday night and held him hostage until Friday afternoon. She struck him a couple times with the butt of a handgun. She tried to get him to make love to her by making him believe she was me."

"Are you serious? Why you?"

"James is in love with me. He has been for a long time, but he hasn't told anybody yet."

"How long have you two known each other?"

"We grew up together and were friends as children, then we drifted apart."

"He often talked about a girl he loved back then; that's you?"

"Yes."

"His good mood makes more sense now. So, what do you want me to do?"

"First, I want things finished, done, and over with Tom. Then I want you to help me with something else."

"What is it?"

"When Tom left the bank with his sister this morning, she said they'd be back for more. I don't want to give him another dime; is there a way to stop their bleeding me for money every chance they get? Also, before Beth left my office, she told Tom she'd also go after James for money because she was sure he had it."

"Courts call that extortion. If she tries to shake James down, we'll take everything we can from her. Prosecutors can bring charges against her and she'll face a substantial jail term. Did Tom have any idea about your new position before today?"

"No, I haven't had the chance to tell him."

"After the judge signed the papers, which should have been the last time he contacted you about supporting him. Let me talk to his attorney and see what she can tell me about this."

"OK. I'll leave that in your hands. Next, I want all these deeds transferred into my name. Then I want the deeds to be set up as part of a trust, so no one can own the estate or the land unless they are direct descendants of John Adams and John Calhoun. I don't want anyone in his family to have access to this inheritance. I'm afraid one of them will try to say I had this when Tom and I were together. If Tom and his sister find out about the estate, they'll try to say it's half his because he was my husband."

"Do you really think they'll try to take the property away from you?"

"Yes, I do. After Tom mortgaged my parents' home, he'd try anything to take whatever I got since we separated."

"Well, then, I will set up the deeds and the rights of inheritance to represent the fact you got this after the two of you separated." "I am building my home out there, and one day, I hope, it will be James's home too. I'm planning a resort on the land that once belonged to John Calhoun. I'll restore the house and create a small town and resort on the property. My dream is for it to be the most wellrespected resort in this area, getting the highest marks for quality.

"Second, I want you to send someone to buy back my parents' house and property in Jacksonville; purchase everything there. I don't care what it costs; just get my parents' home back for me."

Barry did not betray James by telling her it had been him who purchased the property to keep her from losing it. He would simply buy it back and put it into her name as soon as he could.

"Third, I want you to draw up partnership papers between me and James. He will be my business partner in Adams/Calhoun Enterprises. That is where I need your help the most. I want to set up the property in a trust, naming me the executor."

"That's a lot. Anything else you need me to take care of right now?"

"No, I think that should do it. Oh, there is one thing: I need all of this dated for a week after the judge signed mine and Tom's divorce papers. That way, there's no way he can ever come back and say I owned this before we divorced. I can see him using this inheritance to try to get more money, claiming I concealed information to get out of paying him."

"You got it, Tempy. I will take care of everything for you."

"Thank you, Barry."

"You are most welcome. Tell James I said hello and to get some rest. He looks like he could use it."

"I will. See you when you finish the paperwork on all of this."

"I'll call you when it's ready."

"Thank you, Barry."

"You are most welcome. Tempy, thank you for telling me as much as you did about what happened to James and what's going on between the two of you."

"You are welcome. You have been a good friend. But if you want to know any more, just ask James and let him tell you what he wants you to know himself."

"Tempy, can I ask you something?"

"Yes."

"Do you love him?"

"Yes, I do and have for a very long time."

"Does he know?"

"Yes, he does. We already talked about how we feel about each other and what happened to bring him to Pendleton."

"I am glad to hear that. It is about time he can admit who he's in love with. It is also good to hear you feel the same way about him."

Chapter 23

James and Tempy spent as much of their spare time as they could together during Tempy's waiting period. They ate dinner together at either his or her home. Neither of them wanted to be alone, but they could not bring themselves to go any further than kissing and just holding each other. They just enjoyed being with each other. Whenever Tempy was at James's home for the evening, Shawn would come over to do paperwork or to talk.

Barry spent the next two months getting together all the paperwork for the deeds and the partnership. He finished just a few days after Tempy's sixty-day waiting period was over. She was free and could be with whoever she wanted. She could lead the life she wanted and have friends and be happy, all without having to ask anyone for permission.

Tempy could tell James had been having problems with what happened with Evelyn; he was even more standoffish than usual. In the last two months, it felt like their relationship was starting from the beginning. If she called him James, he pulled away from her every time she touched him. But if they were alone and she called him Alex, he was fine. She had no clue what was going on with him, but she was ready to find out. Maybe if she knew what was going on in his head, she might help him get over what happened. It was a frustrating two months, but one afternoon, as they were alone in his office, she called him Alex, and he leaned over and took her hand.

He could be a loving person when they were alone and his guard was not up. He was the man she remembered. But his manner changed as soon as Shawn came back into the office with a client; she had to call him James. She realized at that moment what was happening. James never told her what he and Dr. Smith spoke about during their sessions, but he was aware of what was happening with him, and he wanted to go back to being the old James Braden. He was tired of being confused all the time, not knowing if what was happening to him was fact or fiction. Dr. Smith had been told him repeatedly that Tempy was the key. He recommended that James let the feelings they were having for each other happen. His doctor knew those kinds of feelings had a habit of letting themselves come to fruition at some unusual times. He told him to let nature take its course, and everything will work itself out. If he did not deal with what happened to him, things would never be normal again.

That morning as she drove into work, Tempy decided she was going to move forward with her life. As soon as she got to her office, she asked Brandi to put the bank accounts that belonged to John Adams and John Calhoun into her business name. She filed paperwork with the secretary of state to call her new business Adams/Calhoun Enterprises, with her as the signing partner. Tempy wanted the total in the business account to be five hundred thousand dollars less than what the books showed. She would use part of her inheritance to repay James the money he gave her to settle with Tom. He told her she didn't have to repay the money, but Tempy didn't want to feel obligated.

She was moving forward with her business and her personal life. She planned for these adjustments in her life to be permanent. She was determined to make her new life one she'd be proud of. She was so pleased with plans she was making for her new life and hoped Alex wanted to be a part of that life, but the events of Wednesday through Friday might have caused too much damage to him mentally. Tempy would be whatever James wanted her to be.

During the early morning hours, four months after her divorce was signed, Tempy got out of her nice warm bed and looked in the mirror at the person she had become in the eight months since coming to Pendleton. She could not find herself; gone was the person who feared everything, depended on no one, and could find no peace anywhere she went or with anyone. She felt as though she changed a lot due to events of the last few months. It had been hard waiting the sixty days before she could have a future with Alex or even start an intimate relationship with him. Tom hurt Tempy when he claimed in court she was a slut. She would do nothing to make his accusations seem to be the least bit true.

He was still not over the two days he spent with Evelyn. He was still having nightmares about what she did to him mentally. He found excuse after excuse not to stay in his house. He was only able to stay there a few times since that Friday and would only go if someone went with him. His face and nose healed fine. It was his psychological state Tempy was still concerned about.

They talked a lot about what they wanted. They both could see what lie ahead for them if they could just wait a little while to start a relationship. No one could ever say Tempy left Tom for Alex because before Tempy's divorce was final, and the waiting period was over, nobody knew about her and Alex except the people who were closest to them. The people at the bank knew they had become great friends. Most of them liked the changes they had been seeing in James during those months. He was no longer the recluse he had been before Tempy came to work there. Now he would go into work every morning as the rest of the employees were getting there. He seems to be going back to being his old self, and everybody liked the changes they saw that took place in him.

Tempy and Alex made their sixty-day waiting period plus three additional months before they began seeing each other openly. It took them a while to tell anyone about what was going on with them. When they told other people what was happening between them, everyone was happy to hear it. A few women at the bank thought Tempy and James moved a little too fast, but it was none of their business. They kept most of the intimate details of their relationship to themselves. Stories of the old days were their secrets, and no one else ever would find out about them.

Tempy wanted nothing more than to live her life with Alex in it. She could marry him and introduce him to everyone as the person she loved. Gone was the fear that if anyone found out about them, they'd run back to Tom. He was no longer part of her life, which delighted her.

As she got ready for work that morning, she remembered Alex asking her what she would do with the Calhoun property. She told him she wanted something her family could be proud of for generations to come. She wondered that morning when her other dreams might come true.

On her drive into work that morning, she was thinking about her project in Oconee County. Out of nowhere, at about eleven o'clock, Rick called her and gave her the good news: The resort was on schedule and would be ready in two months. She could not wait to show the world what she had built out there.

Rick also said her house was ready to move into. After almost nine months in Pendleton, she had her own home. No one got it for her; she laid out the floor plans and came up with the interior design. There was one room in the house, however, that only she and Rick knew about. Alex's recreation room was a secret until he was ready to start a life with her.

Tempy met with a client that morning. During the meeting, Rick called her again; he had fulfilled Tempy's wishes by building her the house of her dreams. He had even used the old wooden house that was there when she had inherited the property, incorporating it inside the kitchen and dining room. She was so thrilled about being able to move in, she could not keep from singing. After Tempy hung up with Rick, she called Alex and told him about what they discussed, and her feelings about being able to move in as soon as she wanted to. She hoped he could not hear the longing in her voice. After talking to him a few minutes, she knew what she wanted to do, and she knew how she could get him alone for a little while.

Tempy heard something in his voice and asked, "What's wrong, Alex?"

"I don't want anyone to ruin what we are building, Tempy."

"Have faith, my darling. We can do this together. Remember that. I will see you in a couple of minutes, OK?"

"All right. I am waiting for you."

Before Tempy could get back to the bank, Rick called her back with more good news.

"If you want to, you can walk through the resort this afternoon. I'd like to make sure what we have done up to this point meets your approval."

"OK, Rick, that will be fine. James and I will come out this afternoon. We'll see you around five."

"I haven't seen James in a while; it will be good to see him again. People have been saying James is in a better mood these days. Everybody wants to know what is happening in his life."

"That's a question he needs to answer, not me. But I would give him a little more time before I asked him too many questions; let him adjust to the feelings he is experiencing. I don't want anyone to scare him back into his shell before Shawn and I get him totally out of it. If he does put himself into it again, he will pull himself into it all the way. He took a while to get to the place where he was that isolated person who everyone came to know; it will take him some time to become comfortable again outside the wall he built for himself."

"That's true, Tempy. You're pretty smart. This may not be a good time to say this, but Tempy, if James weren't who you were interested in, I would make a play for you myself."

"Thanks, Rick; that's flattering."

"You are amazing. I hope he realizes just how lucky a man he is."

"Thank you."

"Is he still here?"

"Yes, he and Shawn are in his office, in a meeting."

"Oh, they have their heads together again about something?"

"Yeah, and they said they didn't want anyone disturbing them."

Tempy walked down to Alex's office; she knocked, opened the door, and stuck her head in.

"Hey, you two. Does the 'Do not disturb' order include me?"

Alex looked up and waved her into his office. He shut the door, walked over, and kissed her on the cheek. Tempy wanted more than that, but she was not telling Alex that was not enough anymore. She wanted the whole enchilada, but she didn't want him to know how she was feeling; not yet anyway. She was no longer happy with their decision to take it slow getting to know each other again. She was in no hurry because she knew what she wanted to happen between them. She had been planning it in her mind.

Tempy wanted a life of her own, and she planned on starting that new life as soon as she could get Alex Braden alone. Getting him alone was turning out to be quite a chore. She had been trying to get him alone for two weeks now, and every time she thought she had him where she wanted him, Shawn always showed up. Shawn was always wherever James was, but Tempy had been thinking about this since she got out of bed that morning. With the news Rick had called her about, she now had the perfect way to get Alex away from Shawn. With the house being finished, she had to go to Oconee County to inspect the resort's progress, which fit right into what she wanted to do to get Alex alone and away from the bank and Shawn.

"I came in here to tell you that I will be going out to the property after lunch, to meet with Rick Weber. He told me this morning I can pick up the keys to my new home today."

"It's ready?"

"Rick told me he finished the house. I can come out and inspect it, and if it meets with my approval, I can move in. On my way back to the bank, he called me back and told me he had moved the completion date of the resort up by two weeks. We can also inspect the resort while we are inspecting the house. Oh, I'm sorry; I'm getting ahead of myself. James, will you ride out there with me?"

"Sure, I will. You mean, we will do this together?"

"Yes, that is what I mean. Shawn, is there anything pressing here today that James needs to be around for?"

"No, we have everything well in hand around here. Tempy, you've done a remarkable job since coming here only eight months ago. Both here and at home. In the ten years I've known him, I've never seen him happier.

"Thank you, Shawn. Alex, are we still on for lunch today?"

"Yes, where would you like to go?"

Tempy leaned over and whispered to him, "Your house and the moon. I will cook, and you can just sit and relax for a little while.

"Shawn, you mind if I take him away for the rest of the day while we spend a little time together before we go to Oconee County?"

"No, you two take your time and enjoy yourself. There is not a lot on the calendar for today. He is in good hands with you."

"Thank you."

Tempy walked out of James's office. She turned around at the door and looked at him.

"Are you coming?" she asked.

Alex looked at Shawn and said, "I'll be back later today, I hope. Sounds like I am being kidnapped again."

"Are you all right with that?"

"Yes, a little afraid but I am fine with this, as long as it's Tempy."

"Well then, in that case, we will be fine here. Enjoy your time together."

I wish someone would kidnap me, Shawn thought. I hope that woman carries through with what she has on her mind for him this afternoon. It's about time the two of them find happiness for themselves; they could be happy together.

Chapter 24

James figured out Tempy was up to something, but he was clueless what she had on her mind. It scared and excited him all at the same time to consider what she had going on in that brain of hers. She said she was picking up some steaks at the grocery store, and then she'd be on her way to his house. Tempy hoped this would make all the bad memories associated with his house become just a memory. Maybe she could replace them with good, happy memories.

It had been a long time since he wanted a woman to cook him anything. And he could tell lunch was not the only thing Julia Temperance Brewer was going to try to get a handle on that afternoon. She wanted to be with James; her intentions were to get him alone and show him what she wanted.

James knew this was what he wanted since the day he brought her to Pendleton. When she found out who he was, his feelings only got deeper, but he was still uncertain of himself. To be honest, he wanted this since the day he got to Pendleton.

It had been a long time since he had been with a woman, and James was afraid he would not measure up to Tempy's expectations of him. When he got back to his house, he was more than a little apprehensive about going inside at first, but after a few minutes, he got up the nerve to walk inside. He went in through the kitchen, and on his way in, he picked a bottle wine from the wine rack. As he walked through the kitchen, he took two glasses from the cupboard and carried them into the living room. While he waited for Tempy, he started a fire in the fireplace and put some big fluffy pillows on the floor. He was pouring them a glass of wine when she came in with the steaks.

"You want these now," she asked, "or do you want to wait a little while?"

"Wait a little while," he said. "Come over here and sit beside me."

She took the steaks into the kitchen and put them in the refrigerator. As she came back to the living room, she felt as nervous as a schoolgirl. It had been a long time since she dealt with these kinds of feelings for anyone. She could not remember the last time she daydreamed about someone or had close to the feelings she felt for Alex. She did not want to scare him away, but she was tired of waiting and playing games with him. She realized he wanted his privacy, but she was ready to take this relationship to the next level, beyond what it was when they were younger. She was tired of waiting for him to make the next move.

But Tempy remembered how Taylor was; he wouldn't do anything he wasn't ready for. She promised herself she would show Alex what she wanted from him, that afternoon. She was ready to rekindle their love affair, unless he had no desire to get involved with her. It would disappoint her if he turned her down, but she would understand.

She looked around at what he did with the place while she went to the store. He patted the floor beside him. She walked over and sat down beside him in front of the fire. Her face was warm from the fire, as the blood rushed to her cheeks. She hoped he could not see her blushing; she really hoped he thought the fire caused her flushed cheeks, not him.

"You scared?" he asked.

"A little," she said. "We haven't done this in an awfully long time."

"I'll try to remember the good in what is happening between us this afternoon."

"You mean, you want this as much as I do? Alex, are you sure about this?"

He didn't say a word in answer to her questions; he let his actions speak for him after that. He took his fingers and traced the outline of her lips and framed her face with his hands. He found he could not take his eyes off her, and as he stared into her eyes, she hoped she still met his approval. It had been a long time for them.

Tempy met Alex's gaze and held it; she could see he had taken out his green contacts, and his eyes were blue again, like she always remembered. Those were the eyes she fell in love with. Tempy was finally being allowed to see them again. She stared into his eyes so long, she felt his eyes were consuming her with those big blue pools. She found she was having trouble breathing; she realized at that moment she never wanted another man as much as she wanted Alex, never wanted anyone to touch her the way he did; something was being reignited between them. She wanted to feel like she had when she was a young girl, when he would touch her and hold her close to him. Every part of her body tingled as he held her in his arms

He kissed her on the end of her nose and then at the corners of her mouth. Tempy found the teasing both annoying and exhilarating at the same time. She never said a word, though, she found she could hardly think, and you could forget about her speaking. Forget about getting any words to come out of her mouth. She was in love with Alex Braden; she knew he was Taylor Michaels, but even after thirty years had passed, she still felt the same way.

Alex took the back of his hand and slid it gently down the small of Tempy's back, all the while he was kissing her neck. She felt like putty in his hands. He continued to tease her with his kisses, finally reaching her mouth and kissing her slowly and gently. Even though Alex hadn't been with anyone in a long time, he wanted to go slow and enjoy every moment. She gave herself and her body to him that afternoon in the middle of his living room floor.

He unbuttoned her blouse. He helped her up, and they both took their clothes off. They were standing two inches from each other, but it seemed too far away. Tempy wrapped her arms around his neck and pulled him closer to her. Alex picked her up and held her as tightly as he could. She wrapped both of her legs around his waist, to be as close to him as possible. She had said she wanted them to take it slow and easy, but now she changed her mind. She wanted him. She couldn't think of anything else. The last few days at work were torture; she was thinking of Alex when she should be thinking about the proposals on her desk. She could not add numbers together and had problems performing her job. She needed to find a solution to this preoccupation and hoped to find the answer this afternoon

As they stood beside the fireplace, he kissed her again and then lowered her to the floor. He laid her back onto those big fluffy pillows, moving slowly. He was afraid if he moved any faster, she would make him stop. He kissed her bare neck and then caressed her breasts with his big masculine hands. Tempy rose to meet his touch; she couldn't get enough of the feel of his skin on hers. She had forgotten how well they fit together.

They slipped into each other's arms and were a tangle of bodies on the living room floor. Tempy had wanted this moment to happen ever since the day she figured out who he really was, that first day at the property in Oconee County, but she refused to go too fast for both their sakes. She could feel the heat rising between them and began to run out of breath.

He was having the same problem; he could hardly breathe; he was so excited by her. As they made love in front of the fireplace, he kept repeating her name over and over: "Tempy … Tempy … Tempy."

They never wanted this afternoon to an end. After climaxing together, Alex looked as though years of stress just tumbled off his shoulders. He seemed different, like a new person.

"Alex are you happy?" she asked.

"Yes, I am."

"After Tom's accusations, you still want to be with me?"

"For the rest of my life."

"That's supposed to be my line."

"Well,, that's just how I feel. You make me happy, Tempy. I want to be happy for the rest of my life."

"You don't want other women?"

"No. Remember, I did that all my life; look where it got me. I've tried out enough models. I know which one I want to be with for the rest of my life."

Tempy sank into his arms. They lay on the floor, holding each other, wanting to feel each other for a little while longer. After some time, they and got dressed.

"You ready for lunch?" she asked.

"Yes," he said. "Are you still cooking for me?"

"Yes, I'll cook for you, but you have to promise to behave yourself. We have to be somewhere in a little while."

"I can't promise that Tempy. You bring out the bad boy in me. You always have."

She went into the kitchen to fix lunch for them. She knew if she were having trouble keeping her hands to herself, she could only imagine what he must be going through. Somehow, the two of them got through lunch without too much trouble.

After lunch and an afternoon of lovemaking, neither one of them mentioned what happened before in that house, in that very room. Tempy could see Alex was not afraid to be with her anymore. She did not know what was going through his head, but she saw a smile on his face for the first time since Evelyn tried to take advantage of his feelings for her.

Alex remembered what Dr. Smith said might happen. Tempy might make all the doubts and memories become tolerable for him to live with. He had told him he loved her so much, she was the key to his getting over what had happened. Until they took their relationship to the next level, he might never get over it. As he put his clothes back on, he could feel the fear subsiding, replaced by the peace he had felt with her before. He had not told her how Evelyn used mind control on him and probably never would. He was certainly aware of Tempy being in the room with him. He could finally tell the difference between reality with Tempy and what Evelyn had put into his head.

Tempy knew all about the mind control Evelyn used on him and the suggestions she put into his head. She discussed it with Shawn and even went to see Dr. Smith. She wanted to help him get through this hard period in his life. She was aware Dr. Smith felt she was the key to Alex ever getting over what had happened. She was happy to try to help him in any way she could. Dr. Smith concluded the mind control Evelyn used brought James's desire for Tempy to the surface. That was what James was experiencing, not the mind control but his own desires to be with Tempy.

Chapter 25

After lunch, Tempy walked out of James's house in a daze. She did not hear him when he asked her if she wanted to ride out to the land with him. She was still thinking about what had just taken place. She was so overjoyed, she couldn't contain herself. Alex asked her again if she wanted to ride with him; he wondered if she was afraid for other people to see them together.

She couldn't care less whether people saw them together and said, "Riding with you would be the safer of the alternatives this afternoon."

She didn't think she could concentrate on driving, anyway. Her mind was still somewhere else, and she wanted to be with him as much as she could. She just wanted to spend a little quality time with him before the world came flooding back to them, and they both had to act like adults again.

She and Alex rode out to the estate. When they arrived, Rick was standing at the gate, waiting for them.

"You haven't been waiting too long, have you?" Tempy asked him.

"Not really. I got here a little early so I could walk around before we got started with the inspection."

"You are sure the resort will be ready in the time frame you gave me this morning?"

"I am."

"I can accommodate the number of visitors we spoke about?"

"Yes, about one hundred."

"You've done an excellent job, Rick. I can see you followed what I told you about the buildings around the house. I love how the restaurant is connected to the house by an enclosed hallway. I couldn't open the restaurant to the community if we attached it to the house. I want people to come and enjoy themselves. I want to serve all kinds of meals, from Southern down home to gourmet. I want something for everyone here, with a stable up on the grassy knoll, a zip line, and a pool next to the main house. You think you can get everything ready by then?"

"Yes, Tempy, we got everything you mentioned you wanted at the resort. And let me be the first to tell you, this place is going to outdo your wildest dreams. I think it will be a huge success."

"Thank you, Rick. You have done a magnificent job. Now I can plan the resort's grand opening."

The truth was, Tempy could only think about Alex. She kept thinking about the afternoon they just spent together. She didn't want to go back to work that afternoon and wished this meeting would end so she could get Alex alone.

"Everything looks great, Rick. If you need anything else, just call me at the bank. Alex and I want to walk around the resort by ourselves for a while."

"No problem," Rick said. "Here is my copy of the key and your keys to your house. Just leave my set with my foreman when you leave."

"I'll do that."

"I'll see you two later. I have another appointment in town this afternoon."

"OK, have a safe drive back to Pendleton."

Tempy turned to Alex and said, "You think we would be too obvious if we took the rest of the afternoon off?"

"Tempy, you brazen hussy! Are you going to seduce me out here in the middle of nowhere?"

"Any problem with that?"

"No."

"I have the key to the house. Let's see what we can get into."

"I'd like to get into you, if you know what I mean."

Tempy opened the door, pretending she didn't hear that.

"I wonder what the original owners looked like?" she mused.

The two of them walked around the house for a while. As they walked up to the second floor, Alex noticed the building had a good solid structure, for such an ancient house. As they opened the door to the master bedroom, they were impressed by the condition everything was still in after all those years of just sitting there.

Alex found a cedar chest and opened it; inside were two big fluffy pillows and bed linens. Tempy watched as he took the sheets off the bed and replaced them. Their eyes met as he put the finishing touches on the bed.

Tempy walked over to Alex, standing next to the big bed. She kissed him on the back of his neck, caressed his shoulders, and nibbled his earlobes. As she ran her hand across his chest, the heat inside her was more than she could stand. She took his hand and kissed each of his fingers, one by one. She was no longer afraid of him; she just wanted him to take her in his arms and never let go. She slipped her arms around his waist and slid her hands up and down his back, touching every inch of his skin. She wanted to experience all of him. She unbuttoned his shirt, opened it up, and gently kissed his nipples.

He made a groaning sound deep in his throat. She glanced into his eyes; they were begging her not to quit. She kissed his lips with a fire he had not experienced in years. She wanted to feel every inch of him again and was well on her way to recapturing their intimacy she had missed all those years. She kissed his chest again and then ran her tongue up his neck to his chin.

They took their clothes off right there beside the bed. They wanted nothing between them but air. He lay down on the bed, and Tempy climbed up on top of him, placing one leg on each side of him. They made love in the one hundred-and-ninety-year-old house for the first time that afternoon. Tempy never experienced love like this before, and she had no intention of giving him up now.

He made her feel like an adolescent again. He made her body tingle. She wanted him as close to her as she could get him. They made love for the next hour. Tempy realized she never wanted to be without him ever again. Alex groaned, and his face said it all: He was in heaven. He found what he missed for all those years. She was now making his dreams come true. And based on her reaction, Tempy was as happy as he was.

When they finished, they rolled over into each other's arms and just lay there for a few minutes, holding each other, just staring into each other's eyes; no words were needed to tell each other what was on their minds. Alex and Tempy had given in to their yearning for each other, and he knew that awful time in his life was now behind him. They could move on and be happy.

Chapter 26

Alex and Tempy lay on the big bed, just staring into each other's eyes. When his phone buzzed, they both looked at each other and could not help laughing; they knew it was Shawn. Alex told him he wouldn't be back to the bank that day, and he would see him tomorrow. After he hung up his phone, he turned it off; he didn't want to be bothered for the rest of the day. Tempy had never seen him turn his phone off before. She was aware at that moment she was home. She knew he was where he wanted to be. James could be himself with her. He trusted her not to hurt him.

"I still love you after all these years," he said; he knelt on one knee and said, "Julia Temperance Brewer, we are here in this big, wonderful house, all alone. I can think of no better place on earth than right here and now to do this. Will you marry me?

"Yes, Alex, I will marry you. I have never known another man who affects me the way you do. I can think of no one I would rather spend the rest of my life with."

"Are you answering Alex, James, or Taylor?"

"Alex, when I am with you, I see you. So my answer would be the same for Taylor; if I could marry him, I would. I am well aware of who you are. I have no doubts about my feelings anymore. I love you and want to be with you for the rest of my life."

"Tempy, you made me the happiest man alive again, agreeing to marry me. You made me happy the first time today when you made this happen."

"I have been trying to make this happen for a little over two weeks now, but every time I got close, Shawn would interrupt us."

"I'm sorry, I was not aware you were ready."

"I am just glad we got the chance to be alone and let our emotions catch up with our feelings."

"Me too."

They walked around the old house a little more that afternoon. They stepped through a door in the basement, where they found a secret room. Tempy figured out how to open the door the original builder installed. Inside the secret room, there were trunks stuffed with pictures, letters, and clothes that belonged to John Calhoun and his wife, Sarah, before he and his family moved to Alabama.

Tempy closed the door to that room and decided to have someone from the local museum come out and give her an idea of what this stuff was worth. She didn't want anyone to learn of its contents until she was ready to share it with the world.

She and Alex walked around the estate some more. They walked down to the river and sat down. Tempy was overjoyed, and she was sitting beside the one man in the world who made her happy. She was glad they were spending the day together, alone, no one with them or watching them as they enjoyed each other's company.

They left the river's edge and walked along the path that led to the other house. Alex could see how much Tempy had accomplished since he helped clear the land months ago. They walked up to the house, and she opened the front door. They walked into the empty house together; he could not believe his eyes. It was even lovelier than the house he had built for himself eight years before. He wanted to move in with her as soon as he could. He wanted her to be his wife as soon as possible. In his mind, they had spent enough time apart, and it was now time for them to be together. As far as they were concerned, nothing would ever tear them apart again.

They walked through the house and saw that everything Rick had done was to her specifications. The furnishings showed a lot of taste, and the house was shaping up to be something Tempy could be proud of.

They made love again in the big empty house, and then they began the walk back to the resort. It was a lengthy hike, but they felt they were up to it that day. After a while, Alex stopped and pushed Tempy up beside a huge pine tree and kissed her. They both lost all concept of where they were because of the feelings they had for one another; they made love again next to the tree. Alex thought about how he had manipulated Tempy to get her to Pendleton. Now he was happier than he had been in a long time.

"Tempy, do you ever think about why you came to Pendleton that Monday afternoon?"

"Sometimes I do, but I've heard you and Shawn say a couple of times you led here."

"Does it bother you we manipulated you that way?"

"Sometimes, but if you hadn't, we never would have found each other again."

"Tempy, I loved you even then, and I wanted you near me. Whatever it took, I was going to have you near me."

"I love you too, Alex."

As they walked through the woods back to their car, they could not take their hands off each other. Alex opened the door for Tempy, and she watched him as he walked around to the driver's side of the car and got in himself. As he lowered himself into the seat, he took Tempy's hand in his and kissed it. He held her hand for the entire ride back to Pendleton.

Alex and Tempy arrived in Pendleton about seven that night. Tempy went back to Alex's place, where her car was parked. He wanted her to come in, but she said that making love all day had taken a lot out of her. All she wanted to do was go home, take a shower, and go to bed. Alex would not press; she had already made him the happiest man alive over and over that day. He could wait until another day to have his way with her again.

As Tempy drove home, she called Rick and asked him to move two pieces of furniture out of the plantation house and into her new home: the massive four-poster bed and the cedar chest from the master bedroom. She asked him to move them in before the weekend, when she was planning to move in. She also told him the house was beautiful and built to her specifications. He had done a wonderful job. When Rick completed her house, he could be proud of what he had accomplished. Tempy thought the house was the most beautiful thing she had ever seen, both inside and out.

Chapter 27

Tempy slept like a baby that night. She was happy, and she did not care who found out about it. She found the man of her dreams, and she was on cloud nine. She got up the next morning and took a shower; she should have taken one the night before, but she could not force herself to wash Alex off her. After showering, she walked downstairs to fix breakfast; she was ravenous. Yesterday's events took more out of her than she realized.

She got to the bank by eight thirty, ready to take on whatever came her way. Two loan applications were on her desk. She read them over and found the first one was promising. But the details of the second one made her think the applicant was way out of his league. So she rejected the second one.

About ten o'clock, she strolled downstairs to see if Alex made it in yet. When she got downstairs, Shawn was fretting about Alex not being in yet.

"Hi, Tempy," he said. "I didn't realize you were here. James hasn't come in yet. You got any idea where he might be?"

"Have you tried calling him?"

"Yeah, he doesn't answer his phone."

"I haven't seen him since last night. I was so tired when we got back from Oconee County, I went home and crashed."

Tempy took her cell phone and dialed his number. He answered her after the second ring.

"Hello, babe."

"Alex, where are you?"

"I'm coming into the bank parking lot now. Worried about me, baby?"

"Yes, I thought something had happened to you again."

"It did, but I am all right. I cannot quit thinking about yesterday. Will you have lunch with me today?"

"Yes, I will go to lunch or anywhere else you want me to go with you."

Alex laughed. "I'll be inside in a minute," he said. "Can you do without me for that long?"

"Maybe, but it will be tough."

James laughed out loud again; she could tell he was happy and knew she had caused his change in disposition. She had not seen him this happy before and was glad she took the chance yesterday to show him how much she desired him. Now he knew she wanted to spend the rest of her life with him. She hoped he felt the same way about her.

Chapter 28

James came into the bank through the back door, like he always did, to avoid being seen. He was a creature of habit and had been doing it this way for a long time. It would take a while to get him relaxed enough to be around people again. Tempy and Shawn encouraged him to interact with bank customers on occasion. When he did not want to be around people, Tempy and Shawn were always there, but they knew to leave him alone until he wanted to talk to them. He just could not handle being around a lot of people.

As soon as he got to his desk, he called Shawn and asked him to come to his office for a few minutes.

When Shawn got to his office, James told let Brandi they didn't want to be interrupted.

"Shawn, I asked Tempy to marry me yesterday, and she said yes."

"Jim, that is fantastic news. You have gotten what you wanted from the beginning. That's the reason we did all we did to get her here. I could not be happier for you and for her."

"I went this morning and picked this up for her," James said, opening a jewelry box. "You think she'll like it?"

"If she doesn't, I'll marry you for a ring like that."

Several months ago, James had gone to a jewelry store to have a ring made for Tempy. He ordered a AAA blue tanzanite and diamond ring. The blue stones would knock the socks off any woman.

He told Shawn, "I'm planning to give the ring to her during lunch today."

"I am so glad to hear that. This is great news for both of you. Well, how did yesterday go? From the looks of that ring, I guess that's a dumb question. You have asked her to marry you? And she said …"

"I don't kiss and tell, but I will say it was more than I ever imagined it would be. I haven't been this happy in a long, long time. Oh, Shawn, she said yes."

About ten minutes before twelve, Alex could not wait any longer. He dialed Tempy's extension, but she did not answer. He looked like someone had knocked the wind out of him when her phone just rang. Just as he put his phone down and sat back in his chair, she opened his door and stuck her head inside.

"You ready?" she asked. "I am starving today."

Alex did not know what he'd have done if she changed her mind or went to lunch with someone else. He was so relieved when she stuck her head in his door, he could hardly talk.

"You up to Chinese?" he managed to ask.

"Sure, you know I love good Chinese food."

While they ate, Alex slid his hand into his pocket, pulled out the ring box, and handed it to Tempy.

"I asked you yesterday to marry me without a ring anywhere in sight. I expect this will make up for my oversight."

Tempy took the box and opened it, and with eyes as huge as green saucers, she showed him how perfect she felt her ring was.

"Alex, this ring is exquisite."

"You always said blue was your favorite color. I figured you would like something in your favorite color."

Overwhelmed at the sight of the ring, Tempy began to cry. Alex thought he had done something wrong and she had changed her mind. Tempy assured him she had no intentions of ever changing her mind.

"Alex, you are stuck with me for as long as you want me."

She never expected such a beautiful ring. She promised herself that she'd never let James Alexander Braden out of her sight again.

He slipped the ring on her finger; it fit her perfect.

"I love it, Alex, and I love you."

Chapter 29

Tempy planned to move into her new home the next weekend. She auctioned off the old furniture she brought with her from Jacksonville. She wanted nothing that had been in the house she and Tom had shared. She wanted to be rid of any reminder of her life before she came to Pendleton; her new home reflected her. She filled it with comfortable, modern furniture. After she moved in and made the house her home, she asked some of her friends at the bank to join Shawn and Alex and come over that Sunday afternoon for a housewarming party. To her great surprise, they all said yes. Tempy still had problems believing anyone wanted anything to do with her. For years, Tom told her she was an ugly, second-class person, and no one would ever want anything to do with her. She couldn't count how many friends she made since she left Georgia.

Alex came over that Saturday evening to see what she did with the house. He thought the house looked amazing. She had gotten all the boxes unpacked, and everything looked marvelous. The house looked as though she had been living there for months. She walked into the living room and handed him a glass of wine. She made each of them a sandwich and carried them out onto the back porch. Alex joined her on the porch. They sat in the swing together and began eating their sandwiches; after a minute, Alex reached over, took hers away, and kissed her.

"You want company in this huge house?" he asked.

"I do," she said.

"Can I stay tonight?"

"Tonight, tomorrow, however long you want."

"You want to get married in the living room of this house or someplace else?"

"How about the knoll in front of the waterfall?"

"That's fine with me. I'll marry you wherever you want. Nobody can talk us out of being together ever again."

"I want to do it right this time. I want to remember my wedding day for the rest of my life."

"Then I will make it special just for you."

Alex stayed with Tempy that night. He was surprised to see Rick had brought the huge king-size four-poster bed from the plantation house. That was where they had made love that first day, and she wanted that bed in their home.

They both got up early that Sunday morning and made the house presentable for the housewarming party. Around five thirty that afternoon, people began arriving for the party. She had asked her friends not to bring presents, but many did anyway, and she could not object; she was having the time of her life. As everyone walked around the house, they were amazed at the job Rick had done with the house for her.

She did, however, have a surprise for Alex. As she was showing her guests the house, she showed them a room she had not shown to Alex. As they walked into the basement, she told everyone this was to be Alex's man cave. He did not know she did this. Including the room in her house was a big surprise. She included a pool table, an enormous screen TV, and a bar.

When he saw what she did, he was happier than she imagined. He was on top of the world. He was happy about the room and could not believe how much he cared for this woman. As he looked at what she did with his man cave, he felt nothing but love for her. All he wanted now was to figure out what he could do for her to make her as happy as she made him.

Chapter 30

One week after Rick finished Tempy's home, she moved in and began to get settled. Tempy decided she was going to divide her time between the bank and the resort. She placed an ad for a general manager for the resort and began the hiring process. She spoke with several applicants whose credentials were a close fit for the job. But she couldn't find anyone who filled all her requirements. After a few weeks of searching, however, she found two who came close to matching her requirements. Tempy figured the experience these two had were as close as she would get. One was male, and the other was female. After what happened with Evelyn, Tempy now suspected most women of being secretive and having a hidden agenda. She was cautious with women, and men weren't much better. She found everyone to be unqualified for her resort.

Tempy decided to send both of them an e-mail, inviting them to come in and interview. She scheduled Amy Winters on Monday at nine that morning, and Jonathan Lockhart at one that same day. She still had a lot of positions to hire for and wanted to select a general manager to help her find the right people to staff the resort. First, though, she was looking to find someone who would run her business the way she wanted. The resort was her dream, and Tempy was looking to hire the person who best fit that dream. She was also trying to keep up with her job at the bank. After working on the resort just a few days, Tempy found out just how time-consuming it was getting a resort off the ground.

It was also hard to plan an opening for the resort, trying to make all the arrangements, inviting guests, and arranging the gala. As she worked on one thing, she found she had to do something else. She was running out of time to prepare the festivities and also hire a general manager.

On Monday, Amy Winters arrived for her interview for the job of general manager of the resort on time. Amy did not know she would meet personally with Tempy. Tempy had not even hired herself an assistant to take a little of the pressure off her. She and Amy walked around the resort for about an hour, giving her an opportunity to get to know the resort and a sample of what she might get herself into if she took the job. As the two women talked, Amy discussed her experience in the hotel business; she impressed Tempy with her capacity to make people feel at ease as they talked with her. She always thought of the woman she met her first night in Pendleton and knew she was the type of general manager she wanted for her resort. The two women finished talking; Tempy told Amy she'd make her decision in a couple of days. Amy thanked Tempy for her time and the opportunity she was giving her.

Tempy had about thirty minutes to eat and talk to Alex before her next interview.

"How are you doing with this?" he asked.

"Kind of overwhelmed," she admitted.

"What do you mean?"

"I need someone to deal with all the phone calls and help with making the appointments for applicants to fill all the positions before I can open the resort. I also need time to organize the grand opening and the gala."

"What if I send someone from the bank to serve as your assistant for the time being?"

"That would be awesome; I won't have to worry about making certain they know their job. You'll check them out for me."

"Yes, I will. I love you."

"I love you, Alex. Talk to you in a little while."

After she hung up, Jonathan Lockhart arrived for his interview. He was a slender young man with a cocky attitude. He had blond hair and blue eyes and thought every woman was his captive. They walked around the resort to show him around; he suggested making changes to what she had spent the last year planning. Tempy felt all he wanted was to just get through the interview and take over her business.

"Jonathan, this is my dream," she told him, "And I will run it as though a family lives here. My employees will treat every guest as though they are the only people in the world. If you cannot deal with that, you are wasting my time and yours. My general manager will be in charge of the day-to-day running of the entire resort and answer only to me. But they will run my resort the way I want it run, not the way they want it run. Can you do that?"

"Yes, I can. I have a question for you: Do you have an issue with a good-looking blond-haired, blue-eyed man?"

"No, but my taste in men has nothing to do with what I want for my business."

As they walked back through the lobby, Tempy shook his hand and thanked him for coming. "I will let you know what I decide by the middle of next week."

A little while later, Tempy was sitting at her desk when Brandi Minor walked in the door.

"Hey, Tempy, James said you needed help. I'm here to step in wherever you need me."

"Am I glad to see you. How is Alex?" Brandi was confused by Tempy calling James Alex; she never heard her call James that before.

"Oh, I'm sorry; I've never called him Alex in front of you before. That's my name for James."

"I see."

"Are you ready to get started?"

"Just tell me what you want me to do."

"OK, but it is a lot. It may not seem like much when I tell you, but you will soon get the full picture of what's been going on here."

"Bring it on; between two of us, we'll make this the best resort in the South."

Tempy went into her office and started working on the grand opening; she made a list of officials she wanted to invite personally, including the governor. The grand opening was the weekend before college football started. Tempy knew football season in the South could make or break a business. She wanted to take full advantage of the games. Her resort was in a convenient position for both Clemson and the University of Georgia football fans.

In addition to the governor, she was inviting the mayor of Pendleton, the mayor of Anderson, and the presidents of Clemson and the University of Georgia. She knew it would take her a little time to make all those calls. Alex didn't know it, but sending Brandi to help Tempy meant everything to her. She knew Brandi was Shawn's right hand, but he sent her anyway. She knew he understood the big task in front of her and wanted to help make her resort a smashing success.

Tempy was happy she had help. She asked Brandi to set up appointments for managers of each of the departments of the resort. It would take her the rest of the day and most of the next to go through the resumes Tempy received. Brandi would need several applicants for security, restaurant, entertainment, stables, zip line, movie theater, lifeguards, hotel, lounge, and a mechanic with knowledge of motors, transmissions, and brakes.

To hire a manager, Brandi would need to decide which department needed their experience. After she decided where they could use each one, she and Tempy would sit down and decide who to hire for each position. They would also decide most of the positions with the help of the general manager.

As Brandi was tackling the employee dilemma, Tempy was planning a grand opening for the last weekend of August, with a masked gala planned for the Friday night before. When she got to the resort the next morning, she placed calls to the mayors of each of the cities she had in mind to attend, the governor of the state, and the presidents of both universities lying within fifty miles of the resort. By early afternoon, Tempy had received confirmations from the offices of the high-ranking officials she had invited. The governor of South Carolina called her personally. When she found out that James Braden was her business partner, the governor happily accepted her invitation to attend the gala and the grand opening.

During the next three days, Tempy and Brandi discussed the pros and cons of Amy and Jonathan. They went over both applications until they felt like they knew these two people. Tempy filled Brandi in on the two vastly different interviews she had. She knew from that first afternoon, she preferred Amy over Jonathan, but she was having problems giving in to her gut feeling she was the better candidate for that job.

Tempy thought Jonathan would be a good manager for the security department and decided to offer him that position instead of the general manager's job. If he accepted that position, she and Brandi would have filled two important positions in one day. She called Amy and offered her the position as general manager. To Tempy's delight, Amy responded with an excited yes.

After Tempy got off the phone with her new general manager, she called Jonathan and told him she chose someone else as general manager but thought he would make a fine manager of security, if he wanted it. He said that he would love the opportunity to work for the Adams/Calhoun Resort in whatever capacity Tempy wanted him in.

Tempy worked for three months arranging the gala for the night before the grand opening of her resort. She had planned it as a masked ball with a Southern flair. The invitations specified the event was a masquerade ball, and everyone was to come in their best Southern bell gentleman finery. She had talked Alex into going as Rhett Butler and she was going as Scarlett O'Hara. But she kept one aspect of the gala away from Alex. She had planned it as their wedding reception. While Tempy had been planning the gala, she also organized their wedding, which was on the afternoon before the big event. Tempy was unsure how Alex would feel about the governor being at his wedding, but she was excited about the way things were working out for the grand opening.

Tempy had invited someone else to the wedding and had to tell Alex about it before they arrived. She had asked Bobbie, Alex's cousin from Jacksonville, to be her maid of honor. Bobbie had no clue that Alex was Taylor or that Taylor was even alive. Tempy had to find the nerve to tell Alex about the wedding and explain that Bobbie was coming; she was checking into the resort the next morning. Her heart was in her throat that afternoon, and she was scared to death to tell him. She didn't know how this situation would play out, but she knew she had to tell him that Bobbie would be there the next morning. Tempy was a nervous wreck waiting for her best friend to arrive.

Amy and Jonathan helped Tempy and Brandi go through the many applications they got for the resort's various openings and hired whoever they thought would do the best job. Everyone understood the Adams/Calhoun would be a family place, and staff were expected to treat visitors better than their family would treat them at home. Amy was already turning out to be an asset to Tempy, which allowed her to go back to work at the bank three days a week. Tempy only came in to make sure everything was being done to her liking, and so far, the three people she entrusted with managing the staff had done an outstanding job. By the night before the gala, Brandi, Amy, and Jonathan only had one job left to fill, a technician. Guests to the wedding, the gala, and the grand opening would start arriving the next morning. Tempy was looking forward to the next three days and hoped Alex was not too angry about the surprises she planned.

As she pulled into the driveway that night, Alex's car was already in the carport. She never knew what nights he would come over to stay with her, but she enjoyed it when he did. Alex made that huge house feel like a home.

She walked into the house and called out, "Alex are you here?"

"Yes, I am. I'm in the living room, watching TV. I'd like to talk to you alone for a while; is Shawn coming over?"

"No, he said I should talk to you alone tonight. What's up?"

Tempy sat next to Alex so she could spell out what she had done. She hoped he would not be too mad at her.

"I hope you won't be too mad at me."

"Why, Tempy? What did you do?"

"I planned our wedding for Friday afternoon, and I will use the gala to celebrate the grand opening of our resort and the beginning of our new life together. There's one more thing: I asked Bobbie to be my maid of honor, and she said yes. I haven't decided if I will tell her who you are or not, but she might recognize you."

"Are you kidding me? Are you sure you want to share our secret with anyone?"

"Yes, I know we can trust her, and I want her here with us when we get married. This is what I want. I want to spend the rest of my life with you, but I want one person I can talk to."

"If you are sure, I will be OK."

"Are you mad at me for going behind your back and doing this?"

"No. If this is what you want, I will go along with you. All I want is to spend the rest of my life with you."

"This is what I want most in the world. I got our marriage license yesterday. All we have to do is stand in front of the waterfall at two o'clock on Friday, and the minister and governor will marry us before the gala."

"I kind of like the idea of having our wedding on Friday."

"James Alexander Braden, I love you with all of my heart. All I want to do is spend the rest of my life making you happy."

"Julia Temperance Brewer, you have always been my lover and my friend. I cannot think of anybody I would rather spend the rest of my life with."

After Tempy told him about her plans for Friday, she took his hand and led him upstairs to their bedroom. When they got there, she showed him the suit she had gotten him for the wedding and the suit for the gala. Alex was pleased; all he had to do to be Rhett was wear a nice suit and a mask.

"OK," he said. "You showed me mine, now show me yours."

"All right."

Tempy's gown was dark blue, the intensity of the stones in her ring. She was having her hairstylist fix her hair up like they wore it in the 1800s. After she showed Alex her gown, she took it off and hung it up in her closet. She walked over to the bed where Alex was sitting and began kissing him. He turned around and looked at her in astonishment. Shem didn't have to say another word to him; he knew what she wanted. She and Alex made love that night, and it was both tender and passionate; they wanted to take their time and savor every minute of their lovemaking. They were close to getting what they had always wanted: each other. After they finished making love, they went to sleep that night wrapped in each other's arms. When morning came, Alex kissed her and got ready to leave; he told her he would see her when he got home that night.

After Alex left for the day, Tempy went back to sleep for a while. She knew her resort and its employees were in good hands. She got up about noon and took a shower. When she was done, she went down to the resort to check on the plans for Alex's bachelor party; Shawn had been planning it for weeks. Shawn told her everything was ready; he also told her he would not be coming to her house that night. He'd be partying with the boys.

About five o'clock that afternoon, Alex called Tempy and told her he was going out with Shawn. Shawn had told him it would be his last chance to do anything as a free man. Besides, he'd have to leave Tempy's house before midnight because it was bad luck to see the bride before the wedding.

"I love you, Alex," she said.

"I love you more, Tempy," he replied.

Bobbie checked into the resort a little while later. Tempy had arranged for the staff to give her and her husband a suite. She had sent her a text message before they arrived, asking if she'd like to attend her bachelorette party. Bobbie messaged back that she'd be honored to take part in her joyous celebration.

A little after seven, Brandi called Tempy and asked her if she'd like to have dinner with her and a few friends. Tempy accepted and was happy to not be spending the evening at home alone. Brandi told her to meet her at a nice restaurant on the Oconee River. When she walked in, she saw all her colleagues from the bank and the resort. Brandi whispered something to the host, and a few minutes later, a man wearing a police uniform came out from the back and told them they were all under arrest. She looked surprised, but when the officer started to disrobe and began dancing, she realized he was a stripper.

Tempy was so happy to be there with her friends. She had the time of her life that last night of her freedom. Tomorrow, she would be marrying the man of her dreams.

The next morning, everyone arrived for the festivities of the weekend. Tempy checked the governor and other dignitaries into the resort for the next two nights. Everything was ready, and she hoped everyone loved her new resort as much as she did. It had taken her four months, but the resort was now finished and opened for business. She could not believe people already wanted to experience the resort, and if the reality matched the hype, she was going to have a smashing success with her new venture.

As two o'clock approached, Tempy and Bobbie walked towards the waterfall. She wore a white tea-length gown. Her hairdresser put her hair in a bun with baby's breath to use as an ornament for her veil. As Tempy walked up to Alex, she took his breath away.

Tempy and Alex said their vows in front of the waterfall with their friends and family beside them. She could not believe how many people came to their wedding; they had a lot of friends. She had gotten Alex out of his shell, and he was now socializing with people personally, not just as business acquaintances. Tempy was the best thing that ever happened to him.

As the day wore on, the wedding guests retired to their rooms to change clothes. At eight o'clock that evening, the doors to the ballroom opened for everyone to see what Tempy, Brandi, and Amy had accomplished during the last few months. Tempy had changed her clothes in her office, and Alex changed in a suite so he and Tempy would not see each other. She wanted to be surprised to see what each other looked like when the evening began. As Tempy walked out of her office and stood at the foot of the massive staircase in the resort's lobby, she looked up to see Alex watching her. He made his way to the bottom of the stairs and kissed her.

"You look incredible," he said.

"You don't look bad yourself, Alex," she replied. "You'd give Rhett Butler a run for his money."

"Thanks."

As they stood were chatting, a woman walked up and asked Tempy if she could talk with her. They moved away from Alex and began to speak.

"Yes, what can I do for you?" Tempy asked.

"I am Jane Bohannon, my older sister is Evelyn Bohannon. You might not want to talk with me, but I came here tonight to ask you to help my sister."

"Why would I do that? She held my husband hostage at gunpoint and tortured him for three days."

"Are you sure she held him captive? She's saying it was a consensual relationship."

"That's not how it happened. I'm the one who walked in and found them. I also overheard her telling others she was planning to make James hers by any means necessary."

"That's not the story she's telling her attorney."

"I'd like you to leave the premises before I call security and have you removed."

"We're not going to lie down and let you run over her."

"Either leave or someone will remove you from the premises."

"Can I talk with James?"

"No."

Tempy pulled out her cell phone and dialed the number for security.

"Jonathan, can you please send someone to the lobby?"

"Yes, right away, Mrs. Braden."

A few minutes later, a security guard came into the lobby and walked over to Tempy.

"Mrs. Braden, what can I do for you?"

"I need you to escort this woman to the parking lot. She's not to be allowed back on the premises. Most importantly, she is to have no access to Mr. Braden."

"Yes, ma'am."

The security guard told Evelyn's sister, "Come along with me, ma'am. You're not welcome on this property."

Tempy returned to the gala/reception to find Alex speaking with Shawn and Brandi. She walked up beside him and took his hand.

"Would you like to dance with me?" she asked.

"Sure, I would love that," he said.

"Shawn, I need to talk to you after the grand opening tomorrow."

"OK, do we have an issue?"

"I think so, but we'll handle it."

"OK."

As Tempy and Alex danced, they could not take their eyes off each other. She found him as handsome at fifty-six as he had been at fifteen. Alex was enjoying himself; she could not bring herself to tell him what had happened in the lobby. Guests kept saying they were having the time of their lives. Everyone was dancing and enjoying themselves at the first event of her new endeavor, and it made her heart feel good.

The gala finally wound down, and everyone turned in for the evening. Tempy and Alex went home to begin their lives as husband and wife.

"Tempy, when are we going on our honeymoon?"

"Next week."

"You made all of this happen and kept it a surprise for me?"

"I did. You won't get too mad at me because I did this without asking you?"

"No, I enjoyed myself today. I have not been this happy in a long time."

"Good. Then I accomplished what I set out to do."

After they made love, Tempy and Alex fell asleep in each other's arms. They got up early the next morning and walked up to the resort to go to Tempy's office. Alex could see everyone milling around in the lobby. They stopped and talked with everyone they knew and then walked to the restaurant, where they were shown to their table by the hostess.

After a few minutes, their waitress approached and said, "Hi. What can I get you this morning?"

"Coffee, two blueberry pancakes, and bacon."

"Sounds good," Alex said. "Make it two."

"I'll have your breakfast out in a few minutes."

"Thank you."

While they waited for their coffee, they spoke with the other patrons. Just then, the governor came into the restaurant, and the hostess seated her at a table by herself. Tempy got up and asked the governor if she would like to join Alex and herself.

"Are you sure?" the governor asked. "I wouldn't want to interrupt your first full day as man and wife."

"Yes, we are sure. We have the rest of our lives to spend together. We only get this one chance to make this grand opening special."

"Then thank you, it would be an honor for me to share breakfast with you and James."

She got up and moved to Tempy's table. Afterward, the waitress came back to take the governor's order.

"Coffee, two eggs scrambled, bacon, and toast."

"Thank you; your breakfast will be out in a few minutes."

Alex looked at Tempy when breakfast was over and asked, "Did you notice any issues during breakfast?"

"Yes, I did."

"You going to take care of it?"

"I will, during the regular meeting."

Alex knew she had noticed more than he had; he knew the resort was getting all her attention during the day. After breakfast, everyone went to their rooms and changed clothes. They walked out front at ten o'clock to witness the ribbon-cutting ceremony. While the dignitaries were speaking of the resort and the impact the business would have on the state of South Carolina. Tempy could not help feeling proud of what she had accomplished in the last six months.

After the opening ceremony ended, it was time to have lunch in the restaurant with the governor, before she left to go back to Columbia. Everyone had a relaxing lunch and enjoyed the rest of their day at the resort.

*****

The next day, Bobbie came to Tempy after the wedding and asked her where she and Alex met. Tempy told her she met him after moving to Pendleton. Bobbie could not help worrying about Tempy. She thought she hadn't known Alex long enough and couldn't be sure who he was as a person. She invited Bobbie down to her house, and she said sure.

Tempy and Bobbie walked to Tempy's car and got in; they drove down to the house, where Alex was getting an extra set of clothes for the afternoon. They walked through the kitchen and went out onto the porch and sat in the swing as they talked.

"Tempy, I don't know what it is about Alex, but he seems familiar."

"What's familiar about him?"

"I can't put my finger on it, but I know him from somewhere."

"I think you need to hold on to your seat for this one."

"What do you mean?"

Tempy turned to her, smiled, and said, "Bobbie, that is Taylor. He's alive, he changed his name, and he got a new identity when he left Jacksonville."

"Are you kidding me? His father told Mother he was dead. They held a memorial service for him."

"No, I'm not kidding. He is Taylor."

"Who else knows about this?"

"No one, and he wants me to ask you to please keep his whereabouts between us."

"You know you can trust me."

"Thank you."

"Thank you for telling me he's alive. I love that man with all my heart and missed him to no end."

After Bobbie heard the truth about Alex, she called over to him. He walked into the room with them and sat down.

"Hey, Bobbie," he said.

"Taylor is that you?" she asked.

"Yes, it is."

"I missed you so much. You faked your death?"

"I had to; my life would be in danger if I stayed in Jacksonville."

Bobbie grabbed him and hugged him for a few minutes. He looked at Tempy and could tell she knew he was happy they had told her the truth.

"Bobbie, I can trust you to keep my secret?"

"You know you can. I have kept your secrets for as long as I can remember. This is just like when we were children."

"There is someone else I want to tell, but I don't know how to get him here."

"Andrew?"

"Yes, I would love to see him and talk to him."

"I am so glad you two told me. Let me know if I can help."

"We will."

Tempy had wanted to tell people from his past for a while now. She looked at him and let him know she would take care of Andrew herself. Alex nodded that he would be fine with her getting Andrew to South Carolina.

*****

As everyone was leaving after a fabulous weekend, Tempy was happy about the way most things had gone. She did, however, call a staff meeting to begin in her office for the next fifteen minutes. Before the meeting, Tempy and Alex walked the governor out and thanked her for coming. As the governor got into her limousine, she told Tempy how impressed she was with her and the Adams/Calhoun resort. She also told Tempy the resort would bring many tourists and a lot of revenue to South Carolina. She expected the resort to help the state's economy for a long time. She thanked James for his involvement and his help with the projects that the state had started all over South Carolina with his help. After the governor's limo left, they went back inside the resort.

Tempy walked into her office and began the meeting.

"As you all know, this was a test run to see how the Adams/Calhoun Resort operated. Overall, you passed with flying colors, but a few of you failed. During the next couple of days, you'll be retrained and work with a supervisor to make sure you follow all our policies around here."

As Tempy talked, she overheard one of the waitresses asking her manager who she was.

"Who am I?" Tempy echoed. "Do we have a problem?"

"No, I just wondered why someone who works for the owner had a problem with what we did here today."

"May I ask you who you think the owner is?"

"James Braden, the owner of the bank."

"What made you think Mr. Braden owned this resort?"

"My father said Mr. Braden built this out here."

"Mr. Braden helped finance the development through his bank. He is my business partner, but he does not own the resort. I'm afraid your father is mistaken. I am the owner, and everyone in this room works for me. Anybody who has an issue with that should let me know now so you can find another job."

"We have no issues with it."

"That's good know. I am trusting the running of the resort to Brandi and Amy while I am gone. Every one of you will answer to them when I am not here."

"OK. We will run this resort like you have taught all of us."

After the meeting, Tempy went to find Shawn, who was waiting for Alex in the conference room.

"Shawn, can I talk to you? I have a problem."

"Sure, Tempy, what's wrong?"

"Evelyn's younger sister might create problems for James before we get back from our honeymoon."

"Leave it to me; I'll take care of everything. Go and have a good time and don't worry about the resort until you get back."

"I will. I'm not so much worried about the resort. I am more worried about what Evelyn's family might do while we're out of town."

"Tempy, you and I both know what happened. You'll be testifying against her at the trial. She has no grounds to say she's not guilty."

"I know, but it still doesn't stop me from worrying about him."

"Go have fun. Enjoy your honeymoon."

"Thank you, Shawn. We will call you when we get to our first stop."

*****

"Amy, before Alex and I leave, I need you to do something for me."

"OK, I'll do anything so the two of you have fun on your honeymoon."

"I need you to send a complimentary reservation to John Andrew Brady. You can find his address in my Rolodex. I'd also like you to call him and make sure he can come for a stay after Alex and I get back."

"OK, I will handle it. What if he doesn't want to come?"

"I don't care what you have to do to get him here. We need him here. It is important, and it will be worth his coming."

"All right, I will get him here."

"Thank you."

"You are most welcome."

On Tuesday, Tempy and Alex left for their honeymoon. They spent a month and saw as much of the East Coast as they could. Tempy knew she had hired good people to take care of her dream. She could trust Brandi not to let anything happen to it while they were away. Tempy was hopeful the employees would come to grips with who their employer was. James had not helped her get it. He was just the love of her life and her business partner. Their plans had worked like a dream. Nobody thought she was the owner of anything, and if anybody ever asked, people in Pendleton would say James owned everything.

While Alex and Tempy were on their honeymoon, they made stops in Halifax, North Carolina, and Buckingham County, Virginia, and on their way back, they stopped in Charleston, South Carolina, to see the sites. She and Alex traveled to Niagara Falls and Washington DC; it was a relaxing trip. Alex and Tempy enjoyed the chance to spend time alone, just them for a while. They were due to be back in Pendleton on Sunday afternoon; neither one of them was looking forward to going back to work and back to the way things were before.

They got back to town about nine o'clock that Sunday night. They were so tired, they just wanted to go to bed and sleep for a week, but they had to get up the next morning and go to work.

Alex drove into Pendleton alone. He knew Tempy would follow him, but she had to be back at the resort after lunch. He and Tempy had a board meeting that Monday morning, and after that, she could go back and check on the resort. After the meetings and lunch Tempy drove back to Oconee County.

Tempy got back about two o'clock that afternoon. She walked into the resort and went into her office. While she was sitting at her desk, taking care of paperwork, she noticed that Andrew had accepted the invitation Amy sent him. His reservation was for Tuesday afternoon through Sunday afternoon of that week. He would arrive tomorrow, and Tempy wanted to get things ready for him.

"Amy, I see you scheduled Andrew to arrive tomorrow afternoon."

"He said he'd be glad to accept the invitation to come to stay at the resort. His only request was to bring his two children, and I agreed."

"I was expecting him to bring them with him. Put him in the Owner's Suite when he arrives and call me when he gets here."

"Yes, ma'am, I will handle it."

Tempy had the suite prepared for Andrew's arrival. She would be there when he arrived, but she was still nervous about getting him to the resort. Tempy thought she was ready for Andrew's visit, and she hoped things went the way she had planned. When Alex called her during his afternoon break, she told him Andrew had accepted the invitation and would be in South Carolina Tuesday afternoon.

"Tempy, you know how scared I am about this meeting," Alex said, "but I want to see him and talk to him."

"I know, and I will be with you the entire time."

"I love you, Tempy. Thank you for doing this."

"I love you with all my heart and will do whatever you want me to."

"I'll see you a little after six."

"OK, you want to eat at home or at the resort?"

"Resort; I want you to myself when we go home."

"OK, see you then. Love you."

"Love you too. Bye."

Tempy hung up the phone; she had something to look forward to for dinner and a stack of paperwork to finish. A little after five, her assistant told her she had a call. Tempy sat back and wondered who was on the other end. She took a deep breath and answered.

"This is Tempy, how can I help you this afternoon?"

"Tempy, this is Andrew Brady. I am calling to make sure this invitation for the stay at your resort is for real."

"Yes, Andrew, it is for real."

"OK, we will be there tomorrow afternoon. I am looking forward to a week away. I need a break from everything happening around here right now."

"I will be here when you arrive tomorrow afternoon. Are you still bringing the kids?"

"Yes, and I'd like to bring my uncle with me, if that's OK with you."

"Uncle?"

"One of my uncles helped raise me; he's like a second father."

"That will be fine. I will handle it. Besides, I have put you in a suite with room enough for everyone."

"Thank you for this."

"Andrew, you are most welcome. Can I know the name of the fourth guest?"

"Sure, Taylor Anthony Michaels." At the mention of Taylor coming with him Tempy was scared that things could go terribly wrong.

"OK, we will expect you tomorrow. If you find you can get here a little early, please do so."

After Tempy hung the phone up, she called Amy into her office.

"Amy, there will be four in Andrew Brady's party tomorrow."

"OK, we will have the suite ready for them."

"Oh, God. This will be harder than I thought."

"What's wrong?"

"When I go home, I fear my husband might kill me for what is about to happen."

"You think Alex will have a problem with what is happening?"

"I hope not, but I don't know how he will feel about this."

"You can handle him; he is different when you are with him."

"I hope so."

Chapter 31

The next morning, Tempy told Alex she was going to the resort to meet Andrew when he arrived. She could not bring herself to tell him his father was coming along with him, but she would handle whatever problems they threw at her. She worked through lunch in her office that day. As she ate, she worried about what might happen but then realized she could not do anything about it now. She just hoped Alex could handle the surprise of seeing his father.

Andrew and his party arrived a little after two o'clock that afternoon. Upon their arrival, Amy called Tempy. She came out of her office and walked over to Andrew; when he saw her, his jaw dropped.

"Hi, Tempy," he said. "What are you doing here?"

"Welcome to my resort, Andrew," she said. "You are all welcome to go to your room and get settled. Andrew, could you meet me in the restaurant in about thirty minutes?"

"OK, I'll be there. Should Taylor come with me?"

"I don't want to appear rude, but I need to talk to you alone first."

"OK."

"Believe me, you will understand when we finish."

"OK, now you have my curiosity piqued."

"I will see you then."

"Yes, you will."

Tempy had the bellhop take Andrew and his party to their suite. While they got settled, Tempy called Alex and asked him if he could come home early that afternoon. He told her he could be there about four thirty. She let him know his father had come with Andrew, and she would do whatever he wanted her to.

"Tempy, I trust you. If you think everything will be OK, I will be OK keeping my promise to him. He is aware I am alive, but until now, I have not been able to see him. Thank you for this."

"Baby, I had nothing to do with this. Andrew brought him with him. I will see you then."

"Oh, are you going to talk to Andrew first?"

"Yea, but I still need you here so he doesn't think I'm crazy."

"I'll leave now and be there in a little while."

"Thanks. Bye."

After Tempy hung up, she walked over to the restaurant to meet with Andrew. While she waited, she worked on some of the paperwork that had piled up on her desk while she was on her honeymoon.

About an hour later, Andrew walked in and sat down beside her at the table.

"Hi, Tempy; I am sorry, but I fell asleep."

"That's OK. It gave me time to work on my paperwork and get my nerve up to have this conversation."

"What's up?"

"Andrew, what do you know about Taylor's death?"

"Just that he took an accidental overdose of pain pills."

"Really? You're about to hear a different story."

Just then, Alex came into the restaurant. He saw Tempy and Andrew and went over to her table.

"Tempy, what are you talking about?" Andrew asked.

She looked up at Alex and said, "This is Alex, my new husband."

"Hi, Alex," Andrew said, still looking confused. "Good to meet you."

"Andrew, don't you recognize him? Take a closer look."

"Should I? I don't recognize him."

"Alex, take your contacts out." After he did, she added, "How about now?"

"Wait a minute; are you, Taylor?"

"I am hello, Andrew."

"I was sure something was going on with him, but I didn't have any idea."

"Can you keep this to yourself?"

"You mean I can't tell his father?"

"No, Andrew, he already knows I am alive, but I need you to bring him to our home tonight, so I can see him there."

"You got it."

Andrew and Alex were over the moon to see each other. After they talked for a while, he and Tempy ordered their dinner, and Andrew went upstairs to bring his children and Taylor Sr. down to eat. On their way out of the restaurant, Tempy and Alex stopped by Andrew's table, and Alex told him they'd be at home a little after six.

"We'll be there."

"The young adults can take advantage of all the activities available for the guests at the resort."

"Thanks."

"You are most welcome."

As Tempy and Alex sat on the back porch enjoying the sunset, there was a knock at the door. Alex answered the door and brought the two men out to the porch. He then offered to get them something to drink.

"You want something stronger than tea?" he asked.

"Do you have any Scotch?" Taylor asked.

"I do."

"Make that two," Andrew said.

"Tempy, would you be nice enough to get two Scotches and bring me a glass of sweet tea?" Alex said.

"Sure," she said.

"Don't look like that," Alex told Andrew. "I don't drink alcohol anymore. I am an alcoholic."

"Is it OK if we drink?" Andrew asked.

"Yes, I have lived with this for a long time."

Tempy looked at Taylor Sr. and said, "Mr. Michaels, you don't remember me, do you?"

"Should I?"

"I am Temperance Brewer, and my father was John Brewer. You were in the Air Force together."

"I remember you; it's been a long time. You were a little girl when my wife and I stopped being friends with your parents."

"Taylor, there is no easy way to say what I have to tell you. Do you remember Shawn Mitchell, from the US Marshals Service? He was the Marshal who was in charge of moving Taylor."

"Yes, I do."

Alex walked back in with their drinks at that point.

"He promised you a long time ago to find a way for you to see your son again. Shawn couldn't make that promise come true, but I am about to keep it for him."

"Tempy, how do you know about that promise?"

"What I am about to tell you must stay in this house. Nobody else can ever find out where he is."

Alex handed his father his drink and said, "Daddy, I am Taylor."

"What? No. I always knew you were alive, but Shawn was never able to let me see you. I thought you died."

"Tempy made this happen, Dad."

"Is it OK for you to be talking to us?"

"Yes, nobody knows where I am, and I need it kept that way."

"You got it, son."

Everyone was amazed at how Tempy had pulled this meeting off.

"It was easy," she said. "When you own a resort, you can offer someone a free vacation. It will be easy to keep in touch with you, and nobody ever needs to be the wiser of what you are doing."

"Would you like to come to South Carolina every so often and spend time together like you used to?" Alex asked.

"You bet we would."

"Well, this is the perfect place."

After the three men talked, Alex drove them back to the resort, where they went to their rooms and got settled for the night. When he came back, Tempy had already cleaned up the house and gotten ready for bed. Alex came upstairs and slid into bed beside her.

"Thank you," he said, kissing her. "I love you."

"I love you too. I think you know by now I would give you the world if I could."

"I know. I would do the same thing for you."

They talked for a few minutes and then made love. That night, they found pleasure in just being together.

Over the next five days, the three men were inseparable. They talked Alex into calling Shawn and telling him he would not be coming into work for the rest of the week. Shawn called Tempy to make sure James was OK. When Shawn was sure his friend was OK, he told her not to worry about the bank; he could handle whatever came up. Alex took his father and Andrew hunting, fishing, camping, and horseback riding. Tempy could tell her husband was having the time of his life. She was so glad she could give him this experience.

But like all good things, this one had to end. On Sunday, Andrew loaded his car and got ready for the four-hour drive back to Jacksonville. None of them wanted to go, but they knew they had to. They all promised they would keep in touch with each other. Tempy believed there would be many conversations between them.

"I love you, Temperance Brewer Braden."

"The feeling is mutual," she said. "I love you too, James Alexander Braden."

Chapter 32

Two afternoons later, Tempy was relaxing in her study after she had gotten home from the office. She went onto Facebook to chat with some of her old friends from Jacksonville. She had not been on in a while and was curious to learn what everybody had been up to back home. As she walked upstairs to turn on her computer, she heard Alex come in from work. When she opened her Facebook page, a post from Bobbie caught her eye. She posted some information about Taylor Sr. that caused her to let out the most God-awful scream she ever heard. Without thinking, she shrieked, "Taylor!"

She knew Alex would be watching TV while she checked her Facebook page for any important messages. Ever since they had gotten married and returned from their honeymoon, he would come home from the bank around the same time she did. When he heard her scream, he jumped to his feet. Hex knew something was wrong because Tempy never called him Taylor, not even that first time they made love, not since that first day at that old wooden house, two and a half years ago, when she figured out who he was and called him by his given name.

Alex ran up the stairs, taking them two at a time, to Tempy's study; she was in tears. She balled up in a recliner, clutching her legs to her chest, shaking all over.

"What's wrong, babe?" he asked. "Are you all right?"

She could only manage to point at her computer; it was hard for her to get the words to come out of her mouth, but she finally said, "Alex, we need to talk to Shawn, right now."

"Why?"

"Your father is dying. We need to get home as quick as we can."

"Oh, no. I'll call Shawn and get him out here."

"OK."

Tempy soon calmed down enough to send Bobbie a personal message, asking what else she knew about Taylor Sr.

Bobbie came back with, "His doctors do not expect him to last much longer."

"Is there anything we can do to help him?"

"He wants to see Taylor Jr. one last time before he dies. But he realizes that's impossible and has made peace with the situation. Everyone passes it off as the end stages of life."

Tempy knew this was not the end stages of his life. Taylor was aware his son was still alive and was requesting to see him one last time.

Shawn drove like a maniac to get to Tempy's house. James had informed him of the situation with Taylor Sr., but he had no idea what Tempy wanted Shawn to do. When Shawn arrived at the house, Tempy laid out her plan for him. Alex could never go back to Jacksonville for any length of time, but he could go back for a onetime visit if no one ever learned he was there. His father's condition made it possible to get these two men together. With Taylor Sr. being in the hospital, she had the perfect plan to get Taylor into and out of town with no one ever realizing he had been there.

"Shawn, didn't you promise Taylor Sr. he could see his son one last time?"

"Yes, I did."

Shawn looked at Tempy in complete astonishment. He realized she could arrange for her husband to go back to Jacksonville to have one last afternoon with his father.

"Shawn, if I have to, I will take care of the expenses for this trip myself. Alex deserves to spend time with his father before he dies.

"I need you to go to Jacksonville, go to the hospital where Taylor is a patient. Talk to the administrators about moving Taylor into a private room. After they do, Alex can come into the hospital wearing a mask and gown, and go to Taylor's room."

"That's a great idea."

"Thanks. You and I must continue to keep his secret safe."

"Tempy, I will make it happen. I made a promise to an old man years ago, and now I intend to keep that promise. You and Jim must be ready to go at a moment's notice."

"OK, we'll be ready when you are."

Tempy waited for Shawn to make the preparations, which took forever. She waited for three days, waiting for Shawn to let her know how they would get Taylor into Jacksonville with no one knowing he was there. She could not help fearing that Taylor Sr. would die before he saw his son one last time. She and Shawn were in a race against time. She hoped they would make it before time ran out, but whenever she talked with the hospital administrators, she got the same story. If Alex made it, he could spend time with his father before he passed; if he did not try, he may never forgive himself.

Chapter 33

After a lot of negotiating with the hospital's administration, they allowed Shawn to keep his word. He took a little over four days to make the arrangements to get Alex home. He flew Tempy and Alex back to Jacksonville in a helicopter. Shawn had talked with the hospital several times. The doctors granted them permission to move him into isolation, so anyone visiting Taylor Sr. had to check in at the nurses' station first. This would give nurses an opportunity to keep visitors away while his son was there with him.

Tempy did not know which of his job titles he used, but she suspected his FBI credentials came in handy in this situation. She had never told Alex about Shawn still being an FBI agent undercover to protect him. To this day, Tempy did not know if Alex had not found out Shawn's secret, and Tempy had made a promise that she would never tell.

The helicopter landed at the hospital, and Alex put on the mask and hospital gown. He went through the ER doors and rushed to the elevator. Tempy followed as close to him as she could behind him, down the hallway, to his father's room. James was walking so fast she could hardly keep up with him without running. Once inside, he took off the mask, and for the next thirty minutes, he was Taylor again. Shawn stood guard beside the door just in case someone came by to see Taylor Sr. without first checking into the nurses' station.

"Hey, Daddy, I am here."

"What? Taylor, I thought after your wedding I'd never see you again."

"This woman found out that a friend of ours made a promise to you years ago when you helped get out of a bad situation. She made him honor his promise to you."

"Tempy, how on earth did you find out about me?"

"It was luck. I went online a few days ago and saw a post on Facebook about your condition."

"Daddy, you helped me live, and she had to make your dying wish come true for you. She always thought they should have allowed us to visit over the years."

"How did she know about that, Taylor?"

"I told her about the promise Shawn made you. Bobbie has always been a good friend to her. She sent her a message with the details of your condition and what you wanted before you died. Did you forget she and Bobbie have been friends for years?"

"Yea, I guess I have." His voice was growing weaker and harder to hear with each fleeting moment.

"Daddy, thank you for helping me get out of that horrible situation years ago."

"Taylor, did you ever find what you were always looking for?"

"Yes, sir. I always realized where it was. I could not have it; I made a promise I kept to Mother. Now she is right here beside me. She has been a part of my life for the last year and a half. We got married two months ago and are closer now than we ever were. Tempy makes me happy every day just by being with me."

"Good; it's about time you were happy for a change. Taylor, can you ever come home again?"

"No, Daddy. This is a onetime visit, to help you; no one else can know I was here. Only the four people in this room will be any the wiser about this."

"Thank you, Taylor. I love you, and I always have. Your secret was always safe with me."

"I love you too."

With those words, Alex leaned over to kiss his father's forehead. He realized he gave his father the best present he could have given him. When he stood up, he also realized his father had gone to be with his mother. "Rest in peace, Daddy. Your work here is done."

At that point, the nurses made everybody leave to prepare the body.

Alex did not talk much on the drive back to Pendleton. He was, however, at peace with himself and glad he got to speak with his father one last time. He realized he made his father's last few minutes on earth happy, but that was not enough to take away his sadness. He wept most of the way back to Pendleton and held Tempy's hand close to his heart while he drove. Tempy said nothing to him she sat there and comforted him by being with him. He would let her know when he needed more from her.

Epilogue

Tempy, thank you for what you did for me and my father yesterday. You made a dying man's last wish come true. I now know that all those years ago, my mother and both of your parents were wrong about us. I wish I could revise what happened, but I cannot change the past now. I wish I could, but the past is just that: in the past. We need to make the future the best we can for each other and for those around us.

I have loved you since we were toddlers. We made a daughter together who I never claimed. But I loved her as much as I loved my other two children. I loved you when I ran my car into the side of the ditch across from my home, many years ago. I loved you when you walked into my office, almost two and a half years ago, for a job. I love you more today than words can ever say. You are my best friend and my wife. Tempy, you are the keeper of my secrets; you never sought to hurt me because of them or with them, but a few of my secrets hurt you beyond what any words can ever make go away. My secrets caused you pain without compare, but you still want to be with me. You make me the happiest man alive every day.

When I faked my death, I hoped you would somehow find me. I never dreamed it would happen how it did. I realize nobody from my hometown could know where I was, but I hoped you would find me. When you did, I never thought you would want me back in your life the way I wanted you in mine. I made the circumstances that led to you finding me happen, but if I had to do it over again, I would do the same thing. I wanted you with me; I needed you in my life.

Tempy, you were there during the worst two and a half days of my life. You helped me get over something I thought I'd never come back from. You were strong for me. You proved I could be strong as well and get back some of my self-confidence. You are the person I wanted when we were teenagers, and you are the person I want beside me today. Thank you, Temperance Brewer Braden, for allowing me to mend your broken heart.

I love you, Tempy.

Thank you, most of all, for loving me and for being my wife.